guilty
pleasures

ALSO BY DONNA HILL

Rhythms
An Ordinary Woman
Rockin' Around That Christmas Tree
In My Bedroom
Divas, Inc.
Getting Hers

ANTHOLOGIES

Rosie's Curl and Weave
Della's House of Style
Going to the Chapel
Sister, Sister
Welcome to Leo's
Let's Get It On

guilty pleasures

DONNA HILL

 ST. MARTIN'S GRIFFIN ≈ NEW YORK

This is a work of fiction. All of the characters, organizations, and events portrayed in this novel are either products of the author's imagination or are used fictitiously.

www.stmartins.com

Design by Gretchen Achilles

LIBRARY OF CONGRESS CATALOGING-IN-PUBLICATION DATA

Hill, Donna (Donna O.)
    Guilty pleasures / Donna Hill.
      p. cm.
    ISBN-13: 978-0-312-35423-7
    ISBN-10: 0-312-35423-1
    1. Swindlers and swindling—Fiction. 2. African American women—Fiction. 3. Female friendship—Fiction. 4. New York (N.Y.)—Fiction. I. Title.

PS3558.I3864 G85   2006
813'.54—dc22

                                      2006048106

First St. Martin's Griffin Edition: October 2007

10 9 8 7 6 5 4 3 2 1

*This story is dedicated, with love, to my sister Lisa Hill,
the best friend and supporter a girl could have!
And to my baby bro Dave—don't try this at home! Luv Ya.*

acknowledgments

Big thanks go out to all my writer friends who have been so supportive and inspiring: Leslie (and all her pen names!), Gwynne, Monica (the Web whiz), Lolita, Victoria, my big brothers Vincent and Victor, Francis (for your kind heart), Bernice (I wanna be like you, girl); to all the book clubs and readers who continue to keep me in print (thank you!); my agent, Pattie Steele Perkins, who keeps those checks and contracts coming; my editor, Monique Patterson, who continues to let me spread my wings and grow as a writer; my trio at home, Nichole, Dawne, and Matthew, who keep me humble and in debt! (LOL); my grandchildren, Mahlik and Mikayla, who remind me how wonderful it is to be young; and to Christine, my friend through thick and thin.

Most of all, my thanks to God, who continues to bless me in wondrous ways and who makes all things, big and small, possible.

1

Sex was the nectar that bound them, sticky-sweet and addictive, as addictive as the thrill of the con that drew them together. It was a dangerous game they played. But danger, living on the edge, was who they were, who they'd become—by choice and by circumstance.

For ten years, all of that had been enough. Until Eva Kelly woke one morning and wanted something more, something else. That nagging need sat on the outskirts of her consciousness, nudging her into action. She'd succumbed, but she hadn't told Jake about it. That nagged at her, too—keeping secrets from him.

A cool morning breeze from the open patio door of the hotel room blew across Eva's naked body. Goose bumps rose to attention along her spine. She stirred in her sleep, snuggled closer to the warm, hard body next to her.

Sometime during the night, they must have kicked the

covers to the floor, she thought, drifting in and out of the haze of slumber.

Oh, what a night. Her body still hummed with pleasure. Eva draped her arm across Jake's bare waist. Her diamonds sparkled in the morning light. The slow dance pounding in her chest was her heart, which beat out this rhythm whenever she thought of Jake. A delicious shiver began in her toes and moved sinuously along every muscle of her body.

From the first time she'd spotted Jake in an Atlantic City casino, she knew that something would eventually happen between them, but it wasn't until a year later that they actually met. It was in this very same hotel in Las Vegas that he'd put some kind of mojo on her stuff that had it talking and doing backflips whenever he was in the vicinity. The mere scent of him got her panties wet, and if he smiled . . . well, then it was on. That was ten years ago.

Yeah, she was whipped. No doubt about that. So what choice did she have? She had to marry him, had to ensure that she got what he could give her each and every day. It wasn't only the sex, she reminded herself. She loved Jake. Loved the way he made her feel. Loved the excitement of him that flowed through his veins instead of blood. Loved the double-dangerous life they lived. It was a rush like none other—well, almost. She snuggled deeper. Closed her eyes. Pushed the secret to the back of her mind. Let her thoughts drift.

She'd been on the prowl at the Bellagio Hotel in Vegas, surfing the crowded hotel for the perfect mark. She'd worked the hotels since she was a teenager, out on her own from the age of fifteen. She was good—better than good. She could spot an easy target with her eyes closed. No, she was no whore, not a prostitute. She was a grifter, and a damned good one. Sometimes she considered herself a modern-day Robin Hood, taking from the wealthy to give to . . . well . . . herself. Eva smiled.

There was one thing about the con: one artist could spot another even deep in an African jungle. There was a look in the eyes, like that of a lion choosing its prey from among an unsuspecting herd of animals. The lion is patient, waiting for the moment when the gazelle gets separated from the group. And then *bam!*

They'd kept out of each other's way that time in Atlantic City, marking off their individual territories like two dogs that piss around the perimeters of their spaces. But when they ran into each other again in Vegas, something happened. When her gaze connected with his that night, a half smile of acknowledging challenge curved the right side of his wide mouth. He raised his glass in a subtle toast and winked.

Liquid fire slid down her throat when she swallowed her own drink. Her body grew warm. She ran her tongue across her lips, and her clit struck up a beat like a tiny drum between her legs.

She lost sight of her mark. She didn't care. Jake approached. His walk was fluid, reminiscent of Denzel Washington, a slow, slightly swaying, all-man stride that was full of power and raw sexuality. *Lawdhavemercy.*

Eva leaned with casual calm against the bar—to keep her weak knees from giving out on her.

Jake came up beside her. Resting his back against the bar, he looked out into the crowd. He took a swallow of his drink. "Busy night."

"Depends."

"On what?"

"On how you want to take it."

The scent of him drifted to her. Her pulse kicked up a notch.

"Haven't seen you here before." She turned to the bar-tender and ordered another apple martini.

"Make that two." He grinned at her, watched her from beneath half-shuttered lids. "Now we have two things in common."

"Martinis and what else?"

"I want to take you to bed and you want to go." His hip brushed against hers.

Her pelvis throbbed, needed to press against him. Her gaze drifted up and down his long, lean frame. He was cloaked in all black, devastating. This familiar stranger spewed danger from every pore. His nut-brown complexion, smooth and taut, showed only one blemish: a small scar above his right brow. His chin was square, cheekbones angular to showcase deep-set dark brown eyes beneath a slightly hooded brow. A perfect face, handsome—almost too perfect. She liked the way he held his body, easy and relaxed, comfortable in his own skin. Confident.

"I bet you say that to all the girls." She picked up her second drink and took a long sip.

"Only the ones that appeal to me." He turned sideways to face her profile, then ran a finger along the line of her jaw. He let out a slow breath. "Jake Kelly."

She looked at him. Her insides danced like butterflies let loose. "Eva Davis."

He plucked the drink from her hand and set it down on the counter. He moved so close that she could feel his body heat and the erection that thrummed against her hip. Her eyes remained fixed on his mouth as it moved. He could have been saying anything. Something important. She couldn't be sure and didn't care, so long as she got to taste him.

His features blurred. The faint smell of the martini

drifted beneath her nostrils. The taste of it lingered on his tongue when he slipped it into her partially opened mouth. Just for an instant. So brief, she wasn't sure if the kiss actually happened.

Her lids fluttered open as he came into view.

"I knew it." His voice was husky, intimate.

On a breath she asked him what he knew.

"That you would be sweet." He took her hand. "I'm ready if you are."

He could be Jake the Ripper, she thought absently as she entered his suite that night. He locked the door behind them. But she didn't give a damn as long as she got a little bit of Jake Kelly—then she could die a happy woman.

That night in his room, they didn't just have break-your-back sex, they rewrote the book—leaving them dazed, wary of this thing that erupted between them, and wanting more. Jake did things to her pussy that should have been illegal. It yelped and meowed for hours then purred in satisfaction. Management knocked on the door several times following calls from guests concerned that someone was being hurt.

Jake stirred in his sleep. Eva's memories of that first night faded as she glanced over at her husband and smiled. Ten years as partners, five years as man and wife. They'd certainly had their adventures, she mused, and began to gently stroke his shaft. Even at half-mast, it was lethal. She licked her lips as she felt it grow in her grasp.

Jake moaned, opened his eyes. "What man wouldn't want to be awakened with those expert fingers around him?"

His voice was coated with the veil of sleep, thick and still raspy.

Eva leaned closer. Her strokes grew faster. Jake gripped

the sheet in his fists. His breath hissed from between his teeth.

"Happy anniversary, baby," she whispered before finishing him off in the deep recesses of her hot mouth.

Jake lay sprawled atop the rumpled bed with his hands tucked behind his head. He watched his wife as she moved around the suite, talking about their plans for the day. He loved watching her. He loved everything about her.

Eva was the kind of woman he never thought he'd get. When he saw her that night in Vegas, he knew it was meant to be. Something inside him shifted into overdrive. He hadn't stopped seeing her in his dreams from that evening in Atlantic City. He'd let her get away the first time, but not again. *Screw the con,* he'd thought. In the reflection of her eyes, he saw himself as a horny teenager walking toward her, sure that she'd tell him to get lost, not this dance or any other. But when she opened her legs and let him inside—heaven help him, he was done.

All his life growing up in the belly of urban New York City, he'd drifted in and out of relationships, never staying long enough for anyone to uncover what he really did in his spare time or who he really was beneath the facade. Eva was different. She was a kindred spirit. She understood the art of the game and was ready to play. He'd let her into his life and into his world—at least most of it.

To outsiders, they were simply Mr. and Mrs. Jake Kelly, a young buppie couple living the good life on the Upper East Side of Manhattan. Their three-bedroom town house was like every other in the well-to-do neighborhood. They even had a dog to fill out the picture of domestic bliss. Every day Eva went to work at Sebastian's as a senior clothing designer. Jake used his gift of glib and his looks to sell luxury cars. But their real passion was the con. As a team, they'd mastered it. They were unstoppable and had amassed a hefty sum of money from unsuspecting businessmen—the marks were Eva's specialty.

But over the past few months, she'd begun to lose her edge, her fire. Jake was worried.

"Jake I don't know how much longer I can do this," she'd said about three weeks earlier.

They were in a hotel in Detroit. A convention of CPAs was being hosted there. Eva and Jake were looking over the pictures they were planning to send to the mark's wife.

Jake put aside the Polaroids of Eva in bed with the mark. He looked up at her standing over him. He leaned back in the gilded chair, folded his hands. "Why? We're making more money now than ever."

"It's not about the money." She paced in front of him. He tried to keep his eyes on her face and not on her long bare legs.

"Then what is it?"

She exhaled a breath of frustration, came toward him, and sat down. "I want to settle down, Jake. I want to have a regular life like regular people."

Jake would have laughed, but he could see she was dead serious. "There's nothing regular about us. This"—he waved his hands across the dozen photos spread across the table—"is what we do, baby. It's who we are."

Eva tossed her champagne-colored hair away from her face. "It's not who I want to be anymore. We've been in the game long enough. It's time to get out while we still can."

"Woman, has Rita been in your ear again?"

"Goodtime" Rita Harris was Eva's first cousin, daughter of Eva's deceased mother's sister, who was also long gone.

Rita was a dead ringer for Eva. Those two were thicker than Thelma and Louise. Rita was the party girl of the duo. She'd done time for petty theft, but her specialty was forgery. Her skill was nothing short of genius. He had to give her props. Nonetheless, Rita was the last person that Eva should be listening to, but Rita was about the only person Eva considered a confidante.

"Rita hasn't said a word to me." She rolled her eyes. "If anything, she'd want me to stay in the game so I can keep buying her those designer gifts that she loves."

Jake smiled. That was true. Goodtime Rita loved jewelry and clothes almost as much as she loved crafting the perfect identity papers.

"All right, so it wasn't Rita." He looked her over, searching for some hint in her body language, but it was uncharacteristically rigid. He got up from the table, came around, and stood in front of her. The heat from her body warmed his veins like good brandy. He stepped close enough to hear the sharp intake of her breath.

"Baby," he crooned.

"Jake . . ."

"Damn, I love when you say my name like you need it." He pulled her to her feet and pressed his face against her neck, dragged in a breath. "Love the sound of my name coming from your mouth as much as I like breathing you in."

Her hand crept like vines along his thighs, stroked them up and down. "Jake."

A low rumble against her neck was his only audible response. Jake eased her back against the table, knocked the pictures to the floor with a sweep of his hand.

Hunger whipped its tongue through them with long hot strokes.

Jake pushed up her short skirt, nearly ripping it in his

haste, moved her panties aside, and put two fingers deep into her wet well. The liquid flowed over them.

Eva moaned. Her back arched. She raised her hips and spread her legs wider, opening to him.

They did it right there on top of the table. A scene right out of *The Postman Only Rings Twice* à la Jack Nicholson.

Yeah, he remembered that night in Detroit like it was yesterday. Good to the last drop.

". . . So what do you think, baby?"

Jake blinked, focused on Eva. "Whatever you want to do is cool with me."

She put her right hand on her hip and cocked her head to the side. "You didn't hear a damned word I said." She puckered her lips and waited for him to lie.

He flashed white teeth. "How do you expect me to concentrate with you prancing around here naked?"

Eva arched a brow, took a harder stance.

Jake held up his hands in defeat. "All right, all right. What did you say?"

"I was telling you it would be great if we went sightseeing today."

His face screwed up into a series of wrinkles. "Do we have to?"

Eva refused to laugh at the whining tone. "Yes, we have to. It's our anniversary, and I want to have some fun."

Jake had other plans. The hotel was packed with a convention of bank executives, and he knew they could score big. "I'll go sightseeing on one condition."

Suspicion clouded her eyes. "What?"

He smiled, and she melted against her will, like ice cream left out too long. "Jake . . ."

"Just this last job." He got up and approached her. He put his hands on either side of her waist, his thumbs stroking the undersides of her heavy breasts. "I swear, baby. Just this last time." A hot kiss on her throat, her chin, her lips. Once, twice, longer.

She murmured yes against his mouth.

His fingers teased her nipples to hard pebbles, and it was off to the races.

2

It was lunchtime. The conventioneers swarmed the bar, occupied all the seats in the restaurant.

"Are you sure about this?" Eva whispered as they stood at the entrance.

"Absolutely. Go do your thing. Call me when you're ready."

Eva drew in a breath and sauntered into the dimly lit room. She quickly scanned the occupants, seeking the most likely candidate.

She smiled when she spotted him at the end of the bar. She lifted her chin. The adrenaline charged her like a new battery. If she were a man, she'd have a hard-on. The hunt always did that to her, the equivalent of foreplay.

She approached, pretended to look for someone as she absently took a seat. She brushed against his arm, nearly caused him to spill his drink.

"Oh my goodness. I'm so sorry." She reached for a napkin and patted his chest.

"No harm done." Pale lashes shading paler blue eyes peered at her through horn-rimmed glasses. He held his arms up and away from his plump body as she wiped away the invisible spill.

"I can be so clumsy sometimes. That's what I get for not paying attention." She balled up the napkin, checked his fingers. *Gold band, third finger, left hand. Bingo.* Her eyes flitted over him. A Mona Lisa smile, secret and seductive pulled at the corners of her mouth. "At least let me buy you a drink."

"I . . . I c-couldn't do that."

She noticed his stutter and wondered if it was natural or nerves. "Please." She pressed a bit closer, giving him a whiff of her Dior.

His doughboy faced flushed; the Adam's apple bobbed up and down. "If y-you insist."

Eva leaned in. Her breasts brushed his chest. "I'm sorry. What did you say? It's so noisy in here."

Perspiration dotted his upper lip. "Uh, the d-drink. That would be f-fine."

She turned to the bar, got the bartender's attention. "One more for the gentleman."

Eva leaned toward the mark and in his ear said, "My name is Leslie. And yours?"

"S-Stan. Stan Ingram." He licked thin pink lips.

"Pleasure." The word was a hot puff of air. She felt him shiver. Eva put her purse on the counter and hopped up on the stool, her shirt rising to a dangerous height. "So what brings you here?" she asked, keeping her voice low, forcing him to lean in to hear her.

"Convention," he shouted.

Eva nodded. "You're with the group?"

"Huh?"

She crooked her finger. He leaned his head toward her. She repeated her question.

"Yes. I . . . I a-am."

Their drinks arrived. She raised her glass. "To . . . hmmm . . . new friends."

His pale blue eyes almost sparkled. He clinked his glass against hers.

"So, Stan, what do you do?"

He launched into a banal, mind-numbing monologue about his job at the bank, how long he'd been there, his grandiose plans for the future.

Eva pretended to listen, smiling, nodding and offering the appropriate *hmm umms* in all the right places. In reality, she was doing a quick calculation: ten years at the bank, four as VP of financial securities. He should easily rake in a cool hundred-grand-plus, not including perks. One more thing she needed to check.

"It must be hard on your wife when you have to travel."

He cleared his throat, adjusted his navy pin-striped tie. His cheeks grew rosy. "Lenora unders-stands. S-she knows it's p-part of the j-job."

"That's wonderful. Tell me more." She signaled for another round of drinks.

"Listen, I am so glad you suggested we get out of that bar," Eva said, wrinkling her nose. They walked toward the elevator. "It was so hard to hear you. And your life seems so fascinating. I've never met a vice president before."

He blushed crimson. No one ever complimented Stan Ingram. Most folks generally ignored him, even his wife, of late. To have this gorgeous woman hang on to his every word was the kind of ego boost that Stan only dreamed of. She smelled good, looked good. She didn't laugh at his stutter, but rather at his jokes. No one laughed at Stan's jokes. Not even his wife. This woman was interested in what he had to say. She asked questions. She touched him when she spoke or laughed. No one touched him. Not even his wife. He couldn't remember the last time he and Lenora had a conversation—a real conversation, one that didn't center around her achievements and his lack thereof. Lenora was a beautiful woman too. But her dark-haired beauty had become cold, distant, and calculated. Still, he couldn't let her go. He remained mesmerized by the fact that she'd allowed him into her life, to partake of her bed, to experience the wonders of her body. He was trapped. But while he was with Leslie, he could pretend that none of that mattered.

"We could order room service. I-if y-you're hungry." He swallowed.

Eva turned to him and smiled. "I'm starving." She ran her tongue slowly across her lips.

The elevator dinged. They went up to Stan's room.

This should be over in an hour, tops. Eva followed Stan inside.

Eva tossed their things into the suitcases, squashing Jake's shirts like dirty laundry. Another vacation blown to hell— and their anniversary, at that. She threw eye-daggers at him. He was busy checking the photos. He went over them one by one—a second time, then a third and fourth. Eva slammed a suitcase shut, leaving the sleeves of his good shirt dangling like broken wings.

"Should have gotten this one from a better angle." He held up the picture and scrutinized it again.

Eva took aim and fired. Jake saw the sneaker from the corner of his eye, ducked just in time as it whizzed by his ear.

"Hey!" He held his ear, looked down at the rubber and cloth missile and then at his wife. "What was that for?"

Eva stomped her foot. Her cheeks flared in indignation. "You know good and gotdamned well what that was for, Jake Kelly! You ruined our anniversary—again! Instead of relaxing by the pool with . . . with drinks decorated with little umbrellas, we're running our asses out of here to get on the next plane."

Fury and frustration boiled inside her until they erupted in hot tears that splashed over her cheeks.

"Baby, Eva . . ."

"Don't fuckin' 'baby, Eva' me. Not this time." She balled up his Hugo Boss jacket and dumped it in the next suitcase.

Jake winced. He hated when Eva was upset, especially at *him*. The plane ride home was going to be hell. He and his wardrobe were going to pay.

He dared look at her. "I did it for us. For our security." He slowly came toward her. He held her shoulders. She looked away. "I'll make it up to you. I swear."

Eva sighed. She looked at him then pushed him hard in the chest. "You'd better." The rush of the sting was fading fast.

The knot in Jake's gut released. "You were brilliant, as always." His voice wrapped around her, reeled her in.

A slow smile of appreciation inched across her mouth. "I was, wasn't I?"

"It's in your blood, baby. Just like it's in mine." He grabbed her hips and pulled her between his hard thighs. "It turns you on just like it does for me."

She arched her neck back and drew in a long breath.

"Yesss." Her lids drifted down over her eyes. She lowered her head and then looked up into his eyes.

Damn, he wanted her. A job always did that to him.

"This is the last time, right?" she cooed as she stroked the inside of his thighs. "We're going to take the money and run. Right?"

His heart pounded, pumped blood to his groin. His penis throbbed. He moved against her to gain some relief. "Nobody like you, babe," he said against her neck, his breath like fire on her skin. "Whatever you want."

Eva unbuttoned her blouse. Jake groaned in delight.

"I just have a bad feeling about this, Jake." She sucked in a sharp breath when his tongue teased a nipple. She pulled the black wig off her head and tossed it on the floor.

"Don't be silly." He unzipped her skirt from the back, and it followed the wig. "What could possibly go wrong?"

3

"Hey, Eva," Tara, the office assistant, greeted when Eva walked into Sebastian's design studio Monday morning. "How was your weekend? Did you and Jake celebrate your anniversary in style?"

Eva popped a smile. "It was great. We went to Vegas for the weekend. It's where we met."

Tara grinned with good-natured envy. "You guys are so lucky."

"Yeah, I guess we are." She tossed her handbag over her shoulder and sauntered into her small office.

No one had a clue about her and Jake's other life. They were always careful about taking care of business out of town, away from familiar faces. They'd been lucky. But for reasons that she could not shake, she had real misgivings about this last caper. Maybe she was getting old, sentimental. But, Jake was right. They were masters. Years of success as a team proved it.

Still, she longed for a regular life. He'd promised that this would be their last job. But what if a regular life wasn't enough? This life was all she knew. It was pretty hard to imagine anything else.

Her cell phone rang. It was Jake.

"Got everything together," he said. "It's in the mail."

"Great."

"We'll give Mr. Ingram a call in a couple of days."

"See you tonight."

"Have a great day, baby."

Eva disconnected the call. She twisted her lips. This was it. No turning back now.

TWO DAYS LATER

Stan Ingram ambled into his office. How he hated his job, his mundane life. This was not how he envisioned his future, trapped.

He turned on his computer and opened the files awaiting him on his desk, but he couldn't focus. All he could think about for the past few days was Leslie. The last thing he remembered was taking her to his room and her getting undressed. When he woke up, he was naked and she was gone. The whole episode was a blur. A better description was a *blank*. Had he been able to perform? Was it as good in reality as it was in his mind? *Leslie.*

A sharp knock on his door jerked him back to reality.

"Come in."

"Your mail, Mr. Ingram."

"Thank you, Linda."

She put the mail in his in-box. "You have a meeting at ten."

Stan nodded, reached for the stack of mail, and shuffled through it.

Linda looked at him for a moment, shook her head, and walked out.

Just the usual stuff. Stan tossed the envelopes aside one at a time until he came to a thick brown one. He frowned, reached for the letter opener, and slit open the envelope.

He gasped, grabbed his chest. A handful of color photographs of him, bare-assed naked with . . . Leslie on top, stared back at him.

His stomach rushed to his chest. Bile burned the back of his throat. He blinked hard. Must be some kind of optical illusion, his imagination gone wild.

His hands shook as he picked up the pictures, stared at them in terrified disbelief.

His eyes were closed, but he was smiling . . . or so it appeared. Leslie straddled him. Her naked back faced the camera. Her head was tossed back in a vision of ecstasy. Her black hair hung across her shoulders. Another photo was of him again on his back with Leslie leaning toward his erection, her mouth opened wide.

"Oh my God. Oh m-my God." He grabbed his chest. His heart was out of control. Sweat ran down the center of his back. The room swayed in and out of focus. What did this all mean? Oh God.

The phone screamed. He yelped in shock. He looked at the flashing light. The ring pierced the room again. A wave of nausea loosened his bowels. He reflexively squeezed his butt cheeks to keep from having an ugly accident. Ring!

He forced himself to concentrate, drag his hand toward the phone. He swallowed a nasty taste in his mouth.

"In-g-gram," he stammered. He struggled with his tie, which was choking off his breath.

"Did you get my present?"

His head spun. "I—I don't know what y-you're talking about."

"Oh, I think you do. Maybe you can't talk right now, so just listen. Okay? You have three days to put together fifty thousand dollars in small bills. You'll get a call on day three. Be sure to answer the phone, Stan. I'd hate to have to leave a message. Oh, and one last thing. If you don't have the money, if you don't answer the phone, the next delivery will be to your wife, then your boss, then . . . Well who knows. There are just so many options. Oh, yes, and just like they do on TV, we have copies and a video! Have a great day, Stan. And by the way, you were marvelous!"

Stan Ingram barely made it into the stall of the men's room before his stomach emptied.

Weak and disoriented, Stan made his way back to his office. He locked the door. His mind ran in a million directions at once. What was he going to do? He didn't have fifty thousand dollars, and he had no way of getting it. Lenora controlled all the money; she always had. He couldn't let her find out. Worse, he couldn't let those . . . those pictures get into the hands of management. What little career he had would be ruined.

His intercom buzzed.

He stabbed at the flashing light with his index finger. "Y-yes?"

"Your meeting is starting."

He swallowed. "I'll be r-right there."

Stan sat in his high-backed leather seat, paralyzed by fear and circumstance. He was a fool to have thought that someone like Leslie would have a real interest in him.

Slowly he pushed himself to a standing position. He had three days to figure something out. He shoved the photos in his desk drawer and locked it. Maybe what he should do is simply walk out the bank doors and keep going. Who would miss him anyway?

Lenora Ingram sat in front of her computer. Her emerald eyes studied the encrypted security file on the screen. She'd been working in secret for close to three years to nab Xavier Suarez. It would be her coup de grâce. His capture would garner her the status and recognition that she so richly deserved.

She knew she was loathed within the department. Her nickname among her colleagues was "Little Bitch." Although they dared not say it to her face, she'd heard the whispers and the snickering. All that was about to change, and those snot-nosed bastards would have to *bow down* to the Little Bitch. Suarez was a notorious smuggler, bringing in everything from guns to drugs to diamonds. But the FBI had yet to connect him to anything. He covered his tracks well, and his front men remained equally untouchable. She was getting closer. So close, she could smell his Venezuelan sweat.

She studied Suarez's picture on the screen. He was what romance novelists would describe as devilishly handsome. Of medium height, with dark hair swept back and away from his broad forehead. A thin mustache outlined a rich mouth. His eyes were raven black, piercing, dominated by silky sweeping brows and long lashes. His swarthy good looks belied his ruthlessness. Suarez was said to have murdered his own sister for having crossed him in a drug deal. Lenora wasn't sure if the story was based on fact or urban legend.

She closed that file. This was her personal quest. No one in the department knew what she was doing. It was only a matter of time before she nailed him.

Lenora smiled. She could write her own ticket, get rid of that albatross of a husband, and have the head honchos eating out of her hand. She wondered how they would feel when the tight shoe was on the other foot.

She pulled open her filing cabinet drawer and pulled out the folder containing information on the latest terrorist threat. Her mouth twisted in a petite grimace of disdain. It was all bullshit. A government smoke screen to scare the public. Who the citizens should really be concerned with were their elected officials. *Those* bastards were the *real* criminals.

Lenora took her designer jacket—in the predictable corporate gray—from the back of her hard as nails chair and put it on. For the next hour, she had to listen to the Chief drone on about illegal aliens crossing the borders of Mexico into the United States. She was part of the task force but could give less than a damn about illegals. However, she would play the role for the big boys and bide her time.

"Good morning, Agent Ingram," Mike Fuller said as she passed him in the long corridor. His cool green eyes hungrily took her in.

"Morning, Mike."

He winked. "Nice skirt."

"Fuck you, Mike." She walked off to the sound of his chuckle.

Her department, International Affairs, was run—make

that *overrun*—by men. Men who firmly believed that equal opportunity and women in the work place had led to the downfall of the United States of America. Of course, they didn't speak their thoughts out loud, but it was evident in the sexism and chauvinism in the department. Women were routinely ignored. Most of the female employees were relegated to the secretarial pool, or if they were really talented promoted to the status of Assistant to an Assistant. There weren't even enough women to really protest the treatment. The few who had crawled up the ranks kept quiet and kept their paychecks.

Lenora saw her way out of that fate, and she planned to take it. She opened the door to the conference room, took her seat, and gritted her teeth. It was only a matter of time, she silently chanted. Only a matter of time. She flipped open her notepad and pretended to be interested in the PowerPoint presentation.

When she looked up, the conference attendees were pushing their seats back under the table and gathering their notes.

Lenora shook her head. She'd actually zoned out for the past twenty minutes. She collected her belongings, prepared to leave—when her boss, Special Agent Flannagan, stopped her.

"Lenora, can I see you in my office?" He didn't wait for her response. He walked out of the room.

Several of her colleagues eyed her with curiosity and perhaps a bit of glee. It was a well-known fact that Flannagan never called an agent into his office to ask how the family was doing.

Lenora's eyes darted around the room. She drew in a breath and straightened to her full height of five feet four. She tucked her folders beneath her left arm and walked out.

Moments later, she stood in front of Jerry Flannagan's desk.

"You wanted to see me, sir?"

He dragged his gaze up from the papers on his desk. "Close the door, Agent Ingram."

She did as she was told and came back to stand in front of him.

He reached behind him and turned the wand on the blinds to close them. He faced Lenora. "Now," he smiled slowly. "Get undressed. Get on the couch . . . and spread 'em."

Lenora's green eyes darkened. "With pleasure."

When Lenora walked into her town house in Dupont Circle in the heart of Washington, D.C., the last person she expected to see sitting at the living room table was her husband. Stan never made it home before eight, and it was barely five thirty.

Over the past two years, she and Stan had grown more and more apart. Now when she looked at him, she couldn't find the man she'd married. He no longer excited her. He no longer appealed to her visually. He'd gained weight, was losing his hair, and the slight stutter that she found endearing during the early years grated on her nerves. He'd become stagnant in his job and no longer seemed to have the desire or the balls to claw his way to the top. She'd begun to feel that she was the man in the family. His title of VP of Financial Securities was all bullshit. They both knew it. It was a kiss-off. A way for management to pacify a long-term employee without actually giving him anything worthwhile. She saw her chance to rise to the top, and if it meant doing sexy, freaky things with her supervisor, then so be it. At least she was making the effort.

Lenora placed her briefcase beneath the foyer table, set her purse on top, and walked inside, taking off her suit jacket as she did.

"What are you doing home so early?" She plopped down on the love seat and crossed her legs.

Stan clasped and unclasped his hands.

"Are you all right? Your skin is ghastly pale. Coming down with something?" She looked left and right for her purse, got up, and retrieved it from the table. She fished inside for her pack of cigarettes before returning to her seat. She lit up a Marlboro and blew a long plume of smoke into the air.

Stan screwed up his nose and fought back a cough. He hated smoke. Lenora knew it and refused to quit. He'd once accused her of doing it just to get under his skin.

Stan struggled with his tie.

"What the hell is wrong with you?" Her tiny features pinched into a roadmap of aggravation. "You're fidgeting again."

He placed his hands firmly on his knees. "We n-need to t-talk, Lee."

"Really?" She took a pull on the cigarette and blew out smoke. "About what?"

He started coughing.

Lenora frowned, sucked her teeth, and got up. She returned moments later with a glass of water. Just as she was about to shove it in his hands, she glanced down at the coffee table.

The glass crashed to the floor. The water cut a path across the wood.

Stan raised pleading eyes to his wife's astonished face.

"T-they want fifty-thousand dollars in t-three d-days."

4

Eva strolled along Fifth Avenue during her lunch break, perusing the high-end fashion stores, hoping to spot something in their pricey windows that would be perfect for Rita's birthday. Rita could be a real picky bitch when she wanted to, but Eva loved her to death anyway. It was always a challenge finding just the right gift for a woman who could spot an imitation a mile away.

She was fixing a big birthday dinner tonight and wanted every detail to be perfect, even if Jake's brother Jinx would be in attendance. For reasons that escaped her, Rita and Jinx got on famously. Go figure. He'd tried to hit on her once right before she and Jake got married. She told him if he even dreamed about her, she'd turn him into a eunuch. He'd been a good boy ever since, but she still didn't trust him. She'd never said a word to another soul—*definitely* not to Jake and not even to Rita.

They'd been to hell and back together, Eva mused as she stopped in front of Saks's window. Coming up as young girls with no parental supervision left them to fend for themselves. Neither of them knew their respective fathers. But they looked so much alike, the rumor was that they weren't cousins at all but half sisters, with both of their mamas having laid up with the same no-good man. Neither woman ever admitted as much, though. Rita's mother died of a drug overdose when Rita was six. Eva's mom went to the store one day and just never came back.

Their grandmother, Mary, grudgingly took them in and made it known that they were a burden and she was doing them a favor by putting a roof over their heads and food in their bellies. They did the best they could to stay out of sight and out of her way.

The fact that they'd made it this far was a testament to their resilience. They were survivors. When they turned fifteen, only two months apart, they made a pact that they'd never be poor, hungry, unloved, or caught dead in a bargain outfit again. And to this day, the pact was unbroken.

Eva smiled at her reflection in the Saks store window. She could give Tyra Banks a run for her money. Her shoulder-length hair was intentionally tousled to fall dramatically around her face and across her shoulders. The fitted black turtleneck and black pants gave her a look of sleek sophistication. Her accessories were silver: earrings, chain, wide belt, and matching cuff bracelet.

Hmmm, jewelry. You couldn't go wrong with jewelry. Rita did love white gold. Eva's cell phone chimed. She flipped it open. "Hey, baby." She stepped away from the entrance and pressed a finger to her free ear.

"Just wanted to remind you pick up a bottle of wine on your way home."

"Can't you get it? I'm going to have to race home as it is to get everything done."

"We could have done this at a restaurant, babe. You're making yourself crazy."

"Rita is family, Jake. Didn't I sit through Jinx's arraignment even though I had a deadline at work?"

"You had to bring that up." He gave a good-natured chuckle.

Eva grinned. "I'll pick up the wine if you get your handsome ass home early and put the chicken in the oven. It's already seasoned."

"I can think of much more enjoyable things to do if *both* of us get home early."

Her nipples stood on end. "Jake . . ."

His voice lowered to that sexy timbre that made her crazy. "I was sitting here in my office, with my door closed and a picture of you on my desk, and as much as I tried to fight it, I got a hard-on that could cut glass."

"Jake . . ."

"I'll be home by four. . . . Dinner is at eight. Imagine what we can do in four hours."

A slow smile tugged at the corners of her mouth. "I'll see what I can do."

"That's as good as a promise. Love ya."

She giggled. "Back at ya. And don't forget to put the damned chicken in the oven."

Fortunately she kept an extra pair of panties in her desk drawer, she thought, pushing through the glass doors of Saks. She'd definitely have to change out of the wet ones when she got back to the office.

Eva sniffed the air the instant she walked through the door of their home. She breathed a sigh of relief. The aroma of baking chicken seasoned to perfection filled the air.

"Babe! I'm home and I brought wine," she called out.

Jake emerged from the kitchen wearing nothing but a very short apron.

Eva covered her mouth and giggled. "You look . . . ridiculous."

Jake pressed his hands to his chest. "You wound me, woman. I thought this was kind of a modern-day Olympian look." He glanced down at the apron. "Sorta like a loincloth."

Eva shook her head and laughed some more. "Whatever you say, baby. You'll always be a god in my book."

Jake came up to her, took the package from her hand, and set it down on the coffee table. "Clock is ticking. If we hurry, we can actually take our time." He kissed her behind her ear, caressed her waist.

Eva's eyes drifted closed. "Ooooh, you know that's my weak spot," she whispered.

"Yeah, I know. And this is mine." He took her hand and cupped it over his throbbing erection. "What are you going to do about it?" He unfastened her silver belt.

It dropped to the floor in concert with the ringing phone.

"Damn," he spat. "Probably Rita." He pushed up Eva's sweater.

The phone rang again.

"We better answer," she said, gasping as Jake massaged her breasts, his thumbs running across her nipples. "She'll . . . only keep . . . calling. Ooooh, Jake . . ."

"Let her." He pushed Eva back against the wall, unzipped her pants, and pushed them down her legs. She kicked out of them.

The phone rang.

Eva untied the apron.

"It'll go to voice mail any minute," he said, air rushing out of his lungs.

Eva spread her legs.

Jake lifted her by her hips. Her legs draped around his back.

The phone rang.

He pushed up inside her, and they both cried out.

"You're on fire," he groaned.

"You're so hard. . . ."

The answering machine kicked in. Jake pumped faster. Eva moaned.

"This is Lenora Ingram." They froze. "Yes, Stan Ingram's wife. If you bastards think you can blackmail me and my husband, you have another thing coming. How did I get your private home number? I'm the FB-fucking-I, that's how. And if you two sorry bastards don't want to spend the rest of your thieving lives in the pit of some jail, you'll start playing by my rules. Expect the next call from me. And don't run. I can find you."

Click.

Jake's dick went completely limp and slipped out with a tiny pop.

A perfect dinner sat in the center of the long dining room table. The mouthwatering aromas floated gently around the room. The four diners sat in silence. Jinx twirled his fork.

Rita stared at her French green beans. Jake shifted in his chair. Eva looked at Jake and rolled her eyes.

"I told you I had a bad feeling about this!" She threw her cloth napkin at him. It fell in his plate, right on top of his mashed potatoes and gravy.

He cut her a look from the corner of his eye.

"How do you know this isn't some kinda joke?" Jinx asked.

"Yeah, maybe it's just some friend of his pulling your chain," Rita added. She looked from one to the other.

"They have our private phone number, Rita." Eva took a swallow of her wine.

"So what are we going to do?" Jinx asked.

"We don't know what they want," Jake said.

"I know one thing: I'm not spending a minute behind bars," Eva snapped. "Not even for you, Jake Kelly!" She searched for something else to throw at him, reached for her fork, and tossed it across the table.

"Throwing things at me isn't helping, Eva!" He jumped up from the table and stomped off into the living room. Everyone else followed.

Rita sat down next to Eva and took her hand. "Don't get yourself all twisted," she said softly. "There's nothing we can do until we hear their demands."

"Exactly," Jinx said.

Eva lowered her head. "I don't want to even think about what they may want." She looked at her husband.

Jake paced, getting that bad feeling that Eva had been talking about. "Neither do I."

"The FB-fuckin'-I," they all said in dejected unison.

5

Every time the phone rang for the next two days, Eva and Jake flinched. The third day, it came. Eva answered the phone. Jake picked up the extension in the bedroom when she mouthed *It's them.*

"Listen and listen good," Lenora said. "In three weeks, a shipment of diamonds and a half million in cash will be coming into the United States. You're going to get it and deliver it to me."

"What?"

"No time for questions. Pay attention. The ship is called the *Eleanor.* It's coming in from Brazil. Xavier Suarez will be bringing in the goods himself."

Eva's wide eyes widened even further. *Xavier Suarez. Holy shit.* Suarez was known throughout the underworld as the heir apparent to Carlos the Jackal—the notorious international hit man. Rumor had it that Carlos trained Suarez personally before he was finally captured and imprisoned.

"The boat will dock in Miami. That's your window of opportunity. You'll be receiving a package in the mail in the next few days. That's how we will stay in contact. You fuck up, considered yourselves fucked."

Lenora hung up.

Jake darted out of the bedroom, his eyes as big as balloons. "Did you hear that? Suarez?" He rubbed his brow.

"You got us into this mess. So get us out!" She folded her arms and paced. "This is too awful. I knew we shouldn't have done it. I told you!"

He held up his hand. "Lemme think, will ya. I can't think with you yelling at me."

"Yelling! You think this is yelling? You ain't heard nothing yet."

"How do we know this chick is even for real?"

"She's some-damned-body. She got our very unlisted number. Remember?" Her neck rocked back and forth as she ranted.

"Maybe she works for the phone company."

Eva twisted her lips into a snarl and looked for something to throw. "Phone company employees wouldn't know squat about a diamond shipment coming into the U.S.!"

"Would you keep your voice down? Do you want the whole neighborhood to know we're up the creek?"

Eva huffed, reached for the pillow on the couch, and hurled it at Jake.

He snatched it in midair. "Would you please stop throwing things at me?" he snapped. He returned the pillow to its rightful place and sat down on the couch. He glanced up. "Would you please sit down? You're making me dizzy."

"Good."

"Babe, you were right," he conceded. "Maybe we need to roll up the game board and disappear."

Deflated, Eva sat opposite him on the love seat. "How can we disappear? If she is who she says she is, she'll find us. No matter where we go. We'll be running for the rest of our lives."

"Then we need to find out if she's for real."

"How?"

"Jinx. There's not a computer program he can't crack. If she's really FBI, he'll find out."

"Okay. So when he does find out, what then?"

"We'll deal with it. For now, one thing at a time." He got up.

"Where are you going?"

"To Jinx's house. I don't trust the phone. I'll tell him what we need."

Eva nodded slowly in agreement.

Jake came up to her, kissed her mouth softly. He cupped her cheeks. "We're going to get out of this. I promise."

She swallowed her doubts, needing to believe in her husband. "Hurry back."

While Jake was gone, Eva went over every detail of that night with Stan Ingram. What had she missed? Nothing. Nothing at all. There was no way to tell that he was married to an FBI agent. How was she supposed to know? Maybe she should have asked more questions, but she'd just wanted it to be over, wanted to get out of there and be done with the whole business. She'd slipped the roofie in his drink shortly after they arrived in his suite. As soon as he was good and looped, she called Jake on the cell phone and they staged the photos. Same as they'd always done for years. There had never been a glitch. There had never been a mark who didn't pay, and certainly never one who tried to turn the tables on them. *There's a first time for everything,* some pain-in-the-ass voice whispered in her head.

Eva heaved a sigh. This was all new to her: this feeling of helplessness, being the pawn that was moved around the chessboard. She was accustomed to being the game master, not the other way around. And damnit, she wasn't going to become a pawn now.

She grabbed her purse, car keys, and jacket. While Jake was with his brother Jinx, she needed a powwow with her girl Rita.

Eva smiled as she drove through the city streets. She had begun to formulate a plan. If this chick Lenora was for real, they needed to be ready.

Stan lay in bed next to Lenora. He stared up at the ceiling. He'd been wound tighter than a roll of aluminum foil since he'd confessed the affair to her. After she'd ranted and raved, calling him every kind of fool in the book, she'd made love to him like a woman possessed—the first time they'd been intimate in months. She kept asking all during the act whether "Leslie" was as good as she was. He wished he knew. So of course he told her no. No one was as good as she was. Then after that first night, not another word was said about the incident. When he'd tried to make love to her this evening, she turned her back on him.

She was up to something. It wasn't like Lenora to let anything slide, especially something this big. He turned his head to look at her in the shadows of the bedroom.

How had their marriage come to this? They'd been so

in love once upon a time. They were going to conquer the world together. At first it seemed that they would, but somewhere up the ladder, his foot got stuck in one of the rungs while she kept on going. The higher she rose and the more money she made, the less she seemed to love him. She no longer looked at him with admiration in her eyes, just disdain. So he started to let himself go. It wasn't as if she cared. Maybe he should have left a long time ago. But there was still a big part of him that loved Lenora and ached for her to love him back—again.

He turned his face to stare at the ceiling, folded his hands atop his rounded belly. There was still the matter of the blackmail. Now that he'd told his wife, Leslie—or whatever her name was—didn't have that hold on him, but she'd promised worse. He had one more day to come up with the money.

Lenora's insurance policy was worth a hundred grand. But he didn't have the balls to kill her. He started to sweat. His life had gone from zero to one hundred miles per hour in a blink, and he couldn't even remember if it was worth it.

Lenora's voice came to him in the dark, distant. "You need to plan on taking some time off from work."

"What?"

"You heard me. Put in for your vacation."

Stan pushed himself to a halfway sitting position. "I don't understand."

"You don't need to understand. Just do what I ask, Stan. I'll explain when it's time."

She reached for him. And he was thankful.

When Jake came back home with Jinx in tow, Eva and Rita were sitting in the living room. Jake saw the dark sparkle in Eva's eye, and that wicked smile, and he knew she had a plan.

Now this was the Eva he knew and loved.

They stayed up until the sun was high in the morning sky, planning. Everyone knew what they needed to do. The moment Jinx verified Lenora Ingram's identity, the pieces would begin falling in place. This would be their biggest sting yet, the first time they'd all worked together. If one of them failed, they all failed—and they had no intention of letting that happen.

"Everybody knows what they have to do. Right?" Eva said.

"I'll get cracking on breaking into the FBI files," Jinx said, rubbing his eyes and yawning much too loudly.

Rita stood and stretched. "I'll get started on the documents." She looked at them each in turn. "I'm gonna need recent pictures of everyone. Better yet, y'all go get some new passport photos, and I'll hook them up in Photoshop."

They all nodded.

"We don't have much time," Jake said, looking at his wife. "I'll work on the timeline and getting the schematics for the ship."

"And I'll be getting us outfitted." Eva smiled. She turned to Jinx. "And we're going to need you to get the ship's roster."

Jinx was on it. "Done. Already on my list." He tapped the side of his head.

"Rita, me and you are going to have to do a little shopping for the accessories." Eva winked at her cousin.

Rita grinned. "You know I love shopping."

Jake slung his hands into his pockets. "We got every-thing covered, gang?"

They murmured agreement.

Jake checked his watch. "The clock is ticking, folks. Let's get busy."

6

Eva was in her office. One of her many responsibilities was to oversee the ordering and delivery of materials—from fabrics to accessories—and all the supplies that the designers needed. She dealt with the vendors and manufacturers personally. She was on a first-name basis with them all. That was in addition to supervising the design team and framing the looks for the new season. In some ways, she had to be clairvoyant to see into the future of fashion and try to get there before everyone else. It was stressful, but rewarding to see her vision come to life on the runway and in store windows. More than a few women in Manhattan wore her designs.

She turned on her computer and opened her Excel spreadsheet of manufacturers, dragged in a short breath of apprehension. She had to be sure to cover her tracks. Anything out of the ordinary, and it would all blow back on her.

The entire plan would be shot to hell. Securing the goods was integral to the sting.

Fashion Week was in four months. The designers were deep in the throes of putting the outfits together, working unbelievable hours under incredible pressure. Models were all over the place, coming in for fittings, playing diva, and being general pains in the ass. It was chaotic, to say the least, which is exactly what Eva needed.

There were three vendors in Hong Kong that she could use to get the supplies her gang required. Their stones were exquisite. So good that they had to be taken to jewelers to verify that they were fakes. Timing was crucial.

She opened the file containing order forms, keyed in the information, checked that everything was correct, set the order up as an e-mail, and clicked SEND.

It had begun, the rush. They were going to do a double tap and turn this sting right back on Lenora Ingram's FB-fucking-I ass. She wanted diamonds and money? Eva smiled to herself. She'd get them all right—or at least some damned good replicas. By the time that bitch figured it out, the team would be ghosts. Not to mention the extra little trick they had up their sleeve.

Eva's heart pounded. The familiar hot flush began in the tips of her toes and scooted up her legs. Her pulse rate increased. Her nipples grew hard, and she felt the dampness between her legs. A shudder of need pulsed in the pit of her stomach.

Eva reached for the phone and dialed. "Hey, baby," she said when Jake answered. "Think you can get away for about an hour?"

The tone of his wife's obvious lust gave him an intense hard-on. "You're feeling it too," he stated more than asked.

"When have I ever been able to tell you no? I have a lock on my office door. That's all we need."

Eva grinned. "See you in twenty minutes. I'm leaving now."

"I'm ready."

Eva turned off her computer, snatched up her purse, and darted out.

"Tara, I need to run out for a couple of hours. If any emergencies come up, call me on my cell."

"Where are you going? Sebastian may ask."

"Tell him I had some errands to run, and I'll be back."

Sebastian Long was the owner of the company, the only person she answered to. Sebastian was probably the best absentee employer that any employee could want. Not to mention a brilliant designer. She'd done her apprenticeship under him. However, he did have a habit of calling in or popping up unannounced. But for the most part, he left the running of the day-to-day office activities to Eva. He said he trusted her implicitly, and trust was something that Sebastian didn't hand over easily. Eight years earlier, he'd nearly lost everything he'd begun to build by trusting his then live-in girlfriend, Traci Jennings. Eva never liked her.

Eva'd been with Sebastian when he was working out of his apartment in Greenwich Village. When Traci came along, Sebastian lost all his good sense. Traci was pretty and evil, seeing Sebastian as her meal ticket. He'd let her handle the books and the ordering of materials. Then one day, the orders stopped being delivered, checks started bouncing, and Traci was gone. She'd emptied his bank account, ruined his credit and reputation among his vendors.

It took him more than three years to get back out into the world again. It was Eva who was there, convincing him that he was too talented to let that conniving bitch beat him into submission. Together they pieced the business back together one step at a time. Now they could compete on an even playing field with the best of them.

At the moment, he was in negotiations with an architect to work on designs for a new location. He was expanding the business. If Eva had her way, she would be heading up the new office in SoHo. She smiled.

Sebastian Long was tall, dark-haired, and handsome, with royal blue eyes that were no less than mesmerizing. If she were into white guys, she'd get it on with Sebastian in a heartbeat.

A big knot of guilt tightened in her belly. The last thing she wanted to do was screw over Sebastian. They'd been through so much together. Whatever she needed to do to protect the business and save her neck she would have to do. Somehow she'd find a way to make it all up to Sebastian.

In the meantime, she planned to release this hot flash of desire in the arms of her husband.

Jake walked out onto the sales floor. He could still smell Eva's scent even though she'd been gone for more than an hour. His insides continued to hum as if she strummed him like the strings of a guitar.

No one else could ever understand the chemistry between the two of them. It was beyond explanation. Sometimes the sheer power of it would leave him dazed, bewildered. He would do anything in the world for Eva. Anything. And after this was over, he swore they were out. They'd find someplace to live, start over, have a real life.

He adjusted his tie as he approached a potential buyer.

Running a high-end dealership had pretty much fallen into Jake's lap. Having dropped out of school at an early age and running around with his brother Jinx, he had to find a way to make money. He hopped around from one mechanic's shop to the next, learning the trade, but most of all learning about cars—luxury cars, in particular. He could take an engine apart with his eyes closed and put it back together. He could rattle off a car's attributes and faults just by listening to the motor kick on. He got his first job at sales during the summer of his seventeenth birthday. He was working for a used-car dealer, and he sold more heaps in one month than the owner sold in a year. He knew he had the gift. Being mechanically inclined, he had plenty of opportunity to practice picking the locks of cars, for starters. He worked his way up to doors, safes, alarm systems. There wasn't a security barrier that he couldn't crack. If he couldn't talk his way through a door, he simply broke in—carefully, of course.

"Nice-looking car." He walked up to the middle-aged gentleman.

"I was looking for something for my wife."

Jake relaxed his stance, put on his best smile. "Why don't you tell me a little bit about your wife, and I guarantee I can find the perfect car for her." He patted him on the shoulder and lowered his voice. "And she'll love you for it."

A little more than an hour later, Jake completed the paperwork on a red Mercedes-Benz convertible, two-seater, black leather interior, fully loaded, sleek and sexy. Jake grinned. From what the buyer told him about his wife, he had her beat in age by at least fifteen years. He wanted to keep her happy. That little baby would keep a smile on her face for months.

He filed the paperwork away after confirming with the warehouse that the car would be ready for delivery in seven business days.

Jake reached for the cold cup of coffee on his desk when his cell phone rang.

He pulled it out of his pocket and flipped it open. It was Jinx.

"She's for real."

Jake drew in a breath. "Then it's a go."

"Later, bro."

"Yeah, later."

Jake slid the phone back into his pocket, looked pensively out the window. This was the most dangerous, complex sting they'd ever attempted. Nothing could be left to chance. They all had to walk away from this clean. He'd made a promise to his wife that he intended to keep, and not from behind bars.

Now that Lenora Ingram's identity had been confirmed, they were on the clock. He pulled out his cell and called Eva on hers, telling her about Jinx's confirmation.

"Fine. I already got things going on this end. Barring any holdups, the delivery should be here in the next two to three days."

"Great. What about Rita?"

"I'll give her a call as soon as I get off with you."

Jake puffed out a breath. "Babe, I'm really sorry about this. I should have listened to you."

"Hmmm, you should have, but we won't dwell on it," she said with a hint of humor in her voice. "Hey, there is no way you could have known, and neither could I. I went over everything in my head a zillion times, Jake, and there's nothing I would have done differently."

"All we can do this time out is make sure there are no mistakes. There are too many moving parts."

"Exactly."

"I'll see you at home. I should be in around six."

Eva listened to sewing machines, the barked out instructions, and the grunts of complaints coming from the design floor; then she picked out Sebastian's voice above the fray. "I may have to pull a late one, but I'll get in as soon as I can."

"I'll keep dinner warm."

"Thanks I—" She glanced up. Sebastian was standing in the doorway. "Gotta go, hon." She hung up. "Bass." She stood and came around her desk to greet him in a warm hug. "I didn't expect you today."

Sebastian kissed her on the cheek. "That's one of the perks of being the boss." He held her at arm's length. "You look tired. I've told you a million times to keep those legs of yours closed and get some rest at night." He chuckled at their private joke.

She cocked her head to the side and made a face. "Thanks, Bass." She poked him in the ribs.

"Honesty between friends. That's our motto." He let her go and stepped around her, took a seat on the small sofa in the corner of her office. "So bring me up to date. It looks like Armageddon out there."

Eva laughed. "It's not that bad. You know things are always crazy this time of year." She plopped down next to him, patted his thigh. "How are things with you? How did it go with the architect?"

He tapped out a cigarette from his pack, put it between his lips, but didn't light up. He'd quit six months earlier, and this was all part of his rehab, he'd said. "Hmmm, I wish I could say things went well."

"They didn't?"

"The kind of money he wants, I'll never get the space built in my lifetime."

"Go with someone else."

"I don't have much of a choice. I've already signed a lease for the space for ten years." He ran his hand over his face. "I'll figure something out. I'm going to have to rearrange some funds, cut back on a few things to make it happen."

Eva's insides jerked. "Cut back? . . . Uh, now? We're right in the middle of preparing for Fashion Week." She kept her expression even.

He nodded slowly. "I know. But we're going to have to find a way to trim and still make it all work." He pushed up from the chair. He put the cigarette in his mouth, took it out, and used it as a pointer as he paced in front of her. "Next week we're going to have to do a visual and paper inventory. Look at the forecast sheets and see where we are. Take a look at what's on order and where we may be able to make some cuts."

She swallowed over the dryness in her throat. Cuts. Inventory. Her head pounded. "Sure. But I can take care of that. You need to concern yourself with finding another architect. There has to be someone else out there. Uh, maybe I can start hunting down some designers."

Sebastian grinned. "Always willing to jump in and help. That's why I love you." He leaned down and kissed the top of her head. He straightened. "You have enough to do managing everything and everybody for Fashion Week. I can handle the inventory. I'll pull in Tara to help."

A trickle of sweat dribbled down her spine. "Whatever you think is best. But you know you can count on me."

"I know." He checked his watch. "Gotta run. I have a dinner date."

Eva smiled. "Is she cute?" She winked.

Sebastian blushed. "Very. If things work out, I'll invite you and Jake over for dinner to meet her."

Eva stood and took his hands. "I hope it does work. You deserve someone good in your life."

He grinned; his brilliant blue eyes sparkled. "Yeah. I do, don't I."

She walked him to the door.

"I'll see you next week, and we can get started."

She nodded. "Enjoy your dinner."

Sebastian headed down the short walkway that led to the open studio floor.

Eva squeezed her eyes shut, clenched her fists until her nails bit into her palms. "Shit, shit, triple shit!"

7

Rita had a small workroom set up down the hall from her bedroom. To the casual observer, it looked like your basic office space. But this was where she created her masterpieces. She had three top-of-the-line computers, two scanners, digital cameras, printers, ink, and parchment paper that she had shipped to her from Europe and all the programs most forgers only dream of. She could create anything she wanted, from a simple birth certificate to passports, designer labels to federal identification.

The whole forgery thing was born of necessity. With her mother half-drunk or strung out on drugs most of the time, someone had to put a signature on her school forms, her report cards, permission slips. By the time she was in seventh grade, Rita had a little hustle going. For five bucks, she would forge a parent's signature for a classmate. All she needed was a sample and the money.

She used the money to buy food, keep the lights on, and take Eva with her to the movies on Saturdays. And if they needed something extra, Eva would just pick a pocket or two. Man, that girl was good at lifting wallets, watches, anything that wasn't nailed down. She was the fucking Houdini when it came to making shit disappear.

Rita shut the door to the room and stepped inside, shaking her head and smiling at her train of thought. She removed her robe and took a seat in front of a worktable in her underwear. On the table was a list of all the items she would have to recreate: ship IDs, passports, ship letterhead, and, of course, a suitcase full of counterfeit bills.

The bills would take the longest, and they couldn't look like Monopoly money. She put her headphones on, turned on her iPod, and went to work.

Eva stopped at her favorite wig store on Thirty-fourth Street and purchased wigs for herself and Rita. Then she walked along the streets of the Garment District picking out the accessories that they would need, as well as some additional fabric. After Jinx got the photos of the ship and the crew, she would know better what else they needed in terms of uniform. Nothing could be out of place.

She treated herself to an ice cream cone and headed home with her packages.

Jinx signed for the UPS package and shut the door. Once inside, he ripped open the envelope and dumped the photographs on the table. He smiled and rubbed his hands together. The crew, the captain, the interior and exterior of the ship—it was all there. He took the pictures into his bedroom, where he kept his computer and scanner. He scanned all the photos, imported them into his computer, and then enlarged them. No detail was missed. Eva and Jake would need everything. He printed out the colored photos and put them in plastic sleeves. Damn, it was good to have friends.

Jake looked up when Eva walked in. He hurried over to take her packages. "Whatcha got there, girl?" He kissed her on the mouth.

"Supplies," she murmured against his lips, then walked inside. She looked at the floor plans spread out on the living room table. "I see you've been busy." She walked over to the bar, fixed herself a drink, then brought it to the table. She sat down on the couch and kicked off her shoes.

Jake sat beside her, lifted her legs, and put them up on his lap. He massaged her feet while she sipped her drink.

"The alarm system . . . it's a tough one."

Eva's glass stopped midway. She looked at her husband. His eyes were focused on the lines and boxes on the paper. His jaw flexed. Damnit, if Jake got a case of the nerves, they were screwed.

"Tell me what it is, baby," she said her voice even but firm.

"I . . . I've never gotten into a safe like this one. And I don't have enough time to practice."

"Then you're gonna have to make time. Simple as that." She reached over and took his chin, forcing him to look at her. "This is your thing, baby. It's what you do." She pressed her lips together into a smile. "It's what we do."

He flashed a wicked grin. "Oh, this safe thing," he chuckled, "I figured it out about an hour ago," he lied smoothly, not liking the worry in Eva's eyes. "I'm just going to play around with the mechanisms on the computer. I set up a program."

That much was true. He just hadn't gotten it to work yet.

She reached behind her for a pillow and threw it. "You bastard!"

He snatched it before it made contact with his head, grabbed Eva, and pushed her down on the couch. He stared into her eyes. He could feel her heart pounding against his chest.

"I made a promise to you, and I intend to keep it," he said, inches away from her mouth. "Whatever I need to do to make this happen and get us out in one piece, I'm going to do."

Eva put her hands behind his head and pulled him toward her. "Too much talking . . ."

Jake grinned. He pushed his hand up her dress and pulled her panties down over her hips while she tugged on his belt and zipper.

Their rapid breathing and fits of lusty words and laughter filled the room. Eva draped one leg over the back of the couch and planted the other foot on the floor for leverage. Jake put his hands beneath her and lifted her hips. The head of his penis brushed against her soft hair, and just as he was ready to dive in, the phone rang.

Neither of them moved. The answering machine kicked in, and Lenora's voice stretched across the room.

Jake jumped up, nearly falling headfirst with his pants tangled around his legs. He grabbed the phone.

"Hello!"

"Good thing you answered, Mr. Kelly."

Eva came up alongside him and pressed her ear to the phone, trying to listen.

"Pay close attention. Here are your instructions. . . ."

When Jake finally hung up, he turned to Eva. "She's good."

8

"Okay, so where are we?" Jake asked, leaning back against the couch and taking a long swallow from his bottle of beer.

Every night after their respective day jobs were over the team met at Jake and Eva's house to plan, bringing each other up to date on their progress and sharing any glitches they'd run into.

Eva, Rita, and Jinx sat around the living room table, photos, sketches, and schematics spread out across it.

"The uniforms are just about done," Eva said. "I should be finished in another day or two, and then we can all have a fitting and I can make any adjustments."

Rather than take a chance on pinching fabric from the studio, Eva made her fabric purchases from the wholesale district, using her job identification for the discounts but paying in cash. Each of them needed ship employee uniforms, and they had to be exact—down to the buttons. She worked until the wee hours of the morning sewing the uniforms.

Jake checked uniforms off his list. "What about the switch?"

"The delivery is at the office. I have to find a way of getting them out without anyone noticing. It won't be a problem." She had yet to tell Jake that she had no clue how she was going to be able to take the time off from work. Sebastian would be furious.

Jake nodded and checked that off the list. "What about you, Rita?"

She opened her leather Gucci pouch and pulled out the passports. They all reached for them.

"Wow," Jinx said. He turned his over in his hands and flipped through its pages. "This Paul Young is a world traveler." He grinned. The passport included stops in the Far East, London, Spain, and South America.

"You're an international banker," Rita said, giving him his cover story. "I've prepared some phony documents and letterhead just in case." She handed him a folder that also included a driver's license, ship identification, and a fake credit card. "I wouldn't use that credit card if I were you." She turned to Eva. "The only thing about you that will change is your name: Sylvia London. You're traveling on business. Your ship ID and driver's license are in there as well. Jake, you're a computer salesman. All your identification is there."

They looked over the documents, nodding their heads as Rita spoke. But Rita didn't tell them there was a problem with the money. She'd figure it out. It wouldn't be on her head that this job got blown to hell.

"We're going to be boarding the ship in Brazil," Jake said. "That gives us the entire trip to get the lay of the land, set up, blend in, and pull off this heist. I got us all hooked up with toss-away phones and headsets, real state-of-the-art shit."

Jake had secured all the electronic equipment they would need to stay in contact with each other, from near-invisible headsets to throwaway cell phones. He was still having trouble mastering the mechanisms of the safe without setting off the security alarms. No way he would tell Eva. He was pretty sure he could get the job done. And what she didn't know . . .

"Will we have any time to shop?" Rita asked while she dug in her purse for a stick of gum.

"When we get out of this, I'm going on a month-long shopping spree," Eva said before rolling her eyes at Jake.

Jake winced.

"Are we set with our rooms aboard the ship?" Eva asked, switching subjects.

Jinx nodded. "I took care of it. We'll be going economy. It was the best my buddy could do."

"Who are these 'buddies' of yours anyway?" Rita asked, her brow arched in question.

Jinx grinned. "Trust me, you don't want to know. Some folks I met in the joint. Nice guys, as long as they're on your side."

"And you're sure they won't ask any questions?" Jake probed.

"Naw. As long as their palms are greased, they couldn't care less." He'd sent a special-delivery package to his pal at the Miami PD, with enough cash to send him and his wife on a very nice holiday. He had yet to confirm how they were going to get out of Miami. But he would soon, he hoped.

"This is costing us a pretty penny," Eva said, none too

pleased. They'd spent thousands of their own money on supplies and payoffs, and they weren't nearly done yet.

"The end result will be worth it," Jake said.

Eva cut her eyes at him. "It better be."

Jake rose and stretched. "I guess that should do it for tonight . . . unless there's anything else."

"I need everyone over here next Tuesday for a fitting," Eva said, and then turned to Rita. "Maybe you can meet me at work next week, take some of the stuff out with you. Bring something that's not too conspicuous to carry it all in."

"Not a problem. I'll come by on my lunch break."

"I'll firm up the details with my contact in Miami," Jinx said, picking up his jacket from the back of the couch.

"I'll be glad to get out of here anyway," Rita said, putting on her coat. "The weather here is ready to turn any minute. And you know how much I hate winters in New York. We've been lucky so far."

Jinx got up as well. "Hopefully, our luck will hold out."

"Yeah, we're gonna need all we can get." Eva looked at her husband for reassurance.

"Hey, this is what we've spent our entire lives working toward—the big sting. We'll be ready."

Rita and Jinx said their good-byes, leaving Eva and Jake to face each other.

"Do you really think this plan will work?" Eva asked.

"Your plan is brilliant, babe. Don't doubt yourself." He stepped up to her. "Or me." He placed a soft kiss on her mouth, threaded his fingers through her hair, and held her head in his palm. "I'm not going to let you down, Eva. I promise you."

"It was partly your idea too," she said, her voice whisper soft. "So you can take part of the pain and the glory."

His grin was crooked and endearing. "Absolutely." He

pulled her close and held her, inhaling her scent. "Come on, let's go to bed. We have another busy day tomorrow, and I want to do some more research on Suarez before I call it a night."

They walked hand-in-hand to the bedroom.

"Is he really as dangerous as they say he is?"

"From everything I've read and the inquiries I've made"—he looked her in the eye—"he's worse."

A chill ran up Eva's spine.

9

Lenora was on pins and needles. For days she'd been down-loading her office files to her home computer. With the time off from work to pull off her plan, there was no way she was going to risk having someone else stumble across what she'd been up to. Besides, if things went as planned—which they'd better—she wouldn't be back here anyway.

"Ms. Ingram."

Lenora looked up. Her door was open. Virginia was in the archway.

"Yes, Virginia." She forced a smile on her face. She couldn't stand Virginia. She was a brownnose if there ever was one. She'd been with the bureau for eight years, and all her ass-kissing had gotten her nowhere.

"Agent Flannagan wants to see you."

"Can you tell him I—¿"

"He said, 'Now.'" She smirked. "He was just at my desk."

Lenora muttered something unintelligible beneath her breath. She had to keep up the front to be as annoyed by Flannagan as everyone else was. "Right. I'll be there in a minute."

Virginia walked away.

Lenora leaned back in her seat, bit down on the tip of her pen. Why didn't he just call if he wanted to see her, like he usually did? Jerry could be so damned pompous when he wanted to be. He just had to remind everyone he was in charge.

She sighed and pushed back from her chair. Her affair with Jerry had been going on for the past two and a half years. It started out simple enough. They were working a job together, sifting through the intel following the Trade Center disaster. Daytime hours turned to evenings. Lunch turned to dinner. Dinner to drinks. Drinks to bed. Being in the spy business had worked to their advantage. *Discreet* was the operative word. They were never seen together outside the office under any circumstances. They would decide on a hotel, arrive separately, pay for separate rooms, get together in one room, and then leave the same way they'd arrived.

Jerry was insatiable and very creative. More important, *he* was important. He had the clout to get her where she wanted to go. Yes, she was good at her job, very good, but having an in with Jerry made her ascent up that ladder that much smoother. And the sexual perks were worth the ride. Since their secret affair began, she'd gotten three raises and a promotion. Until this windfall had been dropped into her lap, she'd been focused on staying on track and nabbing Suarez on her own. Then she could kick Jerry to the curb. She'd probably wind up being *his* boss. She smiled at the thought. But now, things had changed.

Lenora logged out of her computer and went to Jerry's office down the hall. She knocked on his door.

"Come in."

Lenora stepped in and closed the door behind her. "What's going on? I was kind of busy."

Jerry looked up. He smiled. "Every time I see you, you remind me of that soap queen, um, um—" He snapped his fingers. "—Erica Kane." He chuckled.

She faked a smile. He'd been telling her that for shit ages. "Really?" But it had taken Susan Lucci—aka Erica Kane—decades to win an Emmy. Lenora, on the other hand, intended to go home with the prize sooner rather than later. She took a seat and crossed her legs, clasped her hands over her knees. "I know you didn't call me in here to tell me how much I remind you of a television actress."

He twitched his mouth to the left then right again. "There is always one thing about you that never fails to tick me off."

"What's that, Jerry?"

"Your mouth. You never know when to keep it closed."

"Is this conversation job-related or what?"

"Your vacation request came across my desk this morning."

She kept her facial expression even. "And? Is there a problem? I have plenty of time."

"Actually, there is."

Her stomach muscles clenched. She hadn't figured on Jerry giving her a hard time about vacation. Had he somehow figured out what she'd been working on and wanted in? "What? I'm all caught up on my work. I'm not attached to any special detail."

He flipped open a file on his desk. "You are now." He turned the folder toward her. "I need you to head up the Task Force."

She pulled the folder closer and scanned the information. Her heart jumped. She was to lead the Task Force on Border Smuggling.

"I want you to get started today. Your budget is substantial, so pull whomever you need. Overtime is preapproved. Do the research. Get the reports written and any investigations. This is a request from the Justice Department. They'll be holding Congressional hearings in a month."

She stared at the paperwork. Her mind worked.

"What's wrong? I'd think you'd be ecstatic. I had to pull a lot of strings to get you on this." His cheeks flushed. His lips thinned into a single tight line.

Lenora cleared her throat and finally looked up. "It's just so unexpected."

Jerry stared at her for a moment. "What else is going on?"

"Nothing. Nothing. Just surprised, that's all." She smiled. "Thanks. Really."

His expression slowly softened. The crease between his brows began to fade. "Is that all the thanks I get?" The corner of his mouth quirked upward.

Lenora licked her dry lips. She got up, locked the door, then returned to Jerry. She wiggled out of her skirt and undergarments, came around to his side of the desk.

Jerry reached out, grabbed her by the hips, and pulled her close.

While Jerry used his mouth and tongue for some deep-sea diving exploration, Lenora moaned on cue and worried about how she would make her little operation happen. This was a glitch she hadn't bargained for.

10

Jake reviewed the ship diagrams. There was no way to be sure if Suarez would use the ship safe or keep the loot in his cabin or, worse, with one of his guards. Suarez was notorious for being a control freak. That could mean two things: either he would keep it constantly under his watchful eye and within reach or he'd keep it secure so an overzealous cleaning woman wouldn't find it in his suite.

With those contingencies in mind, they had to plan for either event. He pulled up the ship security system that he'd downloaded onto his computer, thanks to Jinx.

Jake sighed, rubbed his eyes, and yawned. It was nearly dawn. He'd been at it for hours, but he couldn't risk leaving anything to chance. If they got trapped on that ship . . .

"Baby."

The whisper of Eva's voice came from behind him. He turned with a slow, tired smile.

"Hey."

The short filmy gown she wore snaked over her curves as soft light from the table lamp filtered through it.

She stepped up to him and massaged his shoulders. "You need to get some rest."

"Hmmm," he sighed. Her long fingers kneaded the tight muscles in his neck and shoulders. "I know. I had a few things to go over."

She peeked at the computer screen. "Is that the security system layout?"

"Yeah. It's pretty tricky, but . . ."

"But? But what?"

"But I think we can pull it off." He turned and looked up at her.

"Tell me about it."

"All the doors to the suites are opened by electronic card keys. That part is a cinch. Once we board the ship, you'll have to clip a master card key by posing as one of the cleaning crew staff."

"That's not a problem."

He nodded. "Timing, of course, is key."

"Right. We can't leave too much time between lifting the key, getting into the room, and returning the key before discovery. If that happens, there's sure to be a lockdown on the ship."

"Exactly. And all of the staff, including you, would be subjected to questioning, and ultimately all the key cards would be changed to protect the passengers. The other option: if the stash isn't in the cabin, then it has to be in the ship safe. Getting in there is just as tricky."

Eva pressed her lips together. She released a sigh. "It'll be all right. If not—there will be four black folks jumping ship." She smiled a little.

Jake spun the chair around and pulled her close. He pressed his head against her taut belly.

She stroked his hair. "Are you going to upload all of the floor plans onto our PDAs?"

"Yeah, right before we leave. I want to make sure they're all synchronized, and I don't want to upload them and then possibly have to change anything. I figure two days before we pull out and we'll do a dry run." He paused. "Once we get out of this, babe, it's over. I swear," Jake said.

"We'll go somewhere, start a new life . . ." She stared down at him. "Start a family . . ."

Jake stiffened. "A family?"

Eva pulled back. Her eyes narrowed. "Yes, a family. Me, you, a baby. A family, like on *The Cosby Show*."

Children. In the years that they'd been together, the kind of life they lived didn't have room for children. They'd both understood that, and it had been a tacit agreement between them. For him, that was a good thing. Ideally, he'd hoped that his love would be enough for Eva. He couldn't be a father. It wasn't in the cards. Ever.

"Let's get ourselves out of this first and then see what happens." He stroked her hip, forced a smile.

Eva slowly backed up; disbelief and hurt rocked her. Then without a word, she walked out.

Jake hung his head.

Eva returned to the bedroom and got back in bed. She turned out the bedside lamp and closed her eyes. In the silence of the house, she listened for sounds of her husband.

She folded her hands across her stomach. Family. Since she was a kid, she never knew what that was, what it felt like to live in a loving family. The only semblance of family was what she saw on television.

When she married Jake, sure, they lived a wild life, a dangerous life. For them, children had not been realistic. But in the background, behind the scenes of their double life, there was a powerful love. She wanted to see their love made manifest in a child.

She flipped onto her side. She was getting soft and sentimental. Must be her biological clock ticking. And now was not the time. She knew that. Yet she wanted to have hope, the dream that a *real* life was possible for them.

Jake slipped into the room. He left the door partially open as he'd always done, an old habit he'd carried over from living alone and needing to hear if someone was coming up on him.

The right side of the bed dipped under Jake's weight. Eva moved farther away from him. She curled into a fetal position.

He stole a look over his shoulder. "Eva. We'll work it out. Okay?"

Silence.

"Eva . . ."

No response.

He sighed in exhaustion, got under the covers, and turned his back to her. He tried to sleep.

11

Eva went into the stockroom. She'd stashed her personal shipment of zirconia among the boxes of accessories and supplies. Rita was planning on stopping by during her lunch hour so they could begin removing some of the goods.

Eva went to the back of the room. She frowned as her eyes ran over the boxes. She turned and looked at the row behind her, and her heart pumped faster. Maybe she'd put them someplace else. One by one, she scanned each row of boxes again. Panic seized her. She tugged in a deep breath, and her heart pumped faster. Eva closed her eyes for a moment and then looked again. The three boxes were not there.

For several seconds she stood in the center of the stockroom, chewing on her thumbnail, forcing her mind to clear. Someone had obviously moved them.

"Oh, there you are."

Eva jumped, grabbed her chest. She turned. "Tara, you startled me. Something wrong?" She surprised herself with her calm recovery.

"Sebastian is here. He said he wanted to start going over the inventory with you."

Damnit. She'd hoped that he would have forgotten all about it, with the busy season picking up. "Uh, tell him I'll be right there."

"Sure." Tara hesitated. "Are you okay? You looked flushed."

Eva cleared her throat and rubbed her forehead. "Hmmm, think I might be coming down with something."

Tara stepped back, made a cross with her fingers. "Well, stay away from me, girl. I cannot afford to get whatever it is you think you're getting." She grinned. "I'll tell Sebastian you're on your way."

"Thanks."

Tara started to leave.

"Uh, Tara, I was looking for three boxes that I'd put back here last week."

Tara frowned for a moment and then brightened. "Oh, yes, I have them up front. When I was going over the weekly deliveries, I didn't see those boxes on my spreadsheet or on yours. I was going to send them back, figured it must have been an error."

Eva almost grinned with relief. "Stupid me. I should have transferred the information to your system but totally forgot. I placed that order."

"Oh, okay. Well, I have them up front. Good thing you mentioned it. They were going back today."

"You are just too efficient for your own good," Eva teased.

"I'll bring them back to your office."

"Uh, no. That's okay. Leave them where they are. Sebastian and I will be working in my office for a couple of hours. I'll just be sure to include them on the inventory sheet."

"I can do that for you."

"No," she snapped with more bite than she intended. Tara flinched. "I mean, don't worry about it. You have enough to do if I'm going to be tied up for the next few hours. Plus I need to check them out first. They just might have to go back." She smiled. "I'll get them from you when Sebastian and I are done."

Tara looked at her for a moment, then shrugged. "You're the boss. I'll tell Sebastian you're coming."

"Thanks," she muttered.

When Tara left the stockroom, Eva turned around in a slow circle, her fist pressed to her mouth, trying to think. Now Tara knew about the boxes. She would be looking for them to appear on the spreadsheet. She'd just deal with that later. Maybe it was a blessing in disguise that the boxes were at Tara's desk and not in the stockroom. At least she wouldn't have to worry about Sebastian noticing them there or in her office.

She straightened her jacket and walked out. Now, if she could get through the next couple of hours with Sebastian, she'd figure out the rest. Rita would just have to wait for the pickup until she'd worked everything out on the inside and soothed any suspicions Tara might have.

Tara was young and eager, but she was also willing to please and loyal to Eva. If she'd thought anything was awry, she'd come to Eva before ever going to Sebastian. Of that much Eva was certain. Tara had dreams of running the office if and when Eva moved to the new location. It wouldn't serve her well to get on Eva's wrong side.

Holding on to that small comfort, Eva walked into her office, where Sebastian was waiting.

"I was ready to take a nap," Sebastian teased. He stood to greet her with a kiss on the cheek.

"Bass, you weren't waiting that long." She walked around him. "How are you? Looking good as ever."

"I'm good. Better than good."

"Oh?" Her brow arched in inquiry.

"The young lady I was telling you about—"

She smiled. "The one who is still nameless?"

"Her name is Allison. Allison Hampton."

Eva eyes widened. "*The* Allison Hampton? Of Hampton Enterprises?"

Allison Hampton was the white equivalent of Oprah. She owned two magazines, a radio station, sat on the board of several Fortune 500 corporations, and recently launched her own charitable foundation. She had her hand in any and every humanitarian cause, near and far. That's because she had enough money to pay off the national debt—out of her petty cash. Her father was a senator for decades until he died five years earlier. The family made their first fortune during Prohibition and then legitimized themselves in oil, then turned to stocks. She was an only child and heiress to a megafortune, which, by all accounts, she spent wisely. There'd been rumors that her father had had very close ties with the Saudis, but the speculation was never proved.

Sebastian grinned. "Yes, *the* Allison Hampton."

"Well, you certainly go for the gusto. Congratulations." She stepped closer and lowered her voice. "Are those really her boobs, or does she have a good surgeon?"

Sebastian tossed his head back and howled with laughter. "I'll let you know. How's that?"

Eva chuckled. "As long as you're happy. I just hope she treats you nice. Or else you know she will be subject to a beatdown. I don't care how much money she has."

"I'm a big boy, Eva. I can take care of myself. But I appreciate your sentiments."

She wagged a finger at him. "Listen, you know all you have to do is put your lips together and blow. I'll be there."

He shook his head in merriment. "I'll keep that in mind."

"So . . . I take it the date went well?"

"Yes, very. The first, and every one since then too. We've been seeing each other practically every night."

"Wow. This does sound serious."

Sebastian sat down. He looked up at Eva. "I think so. At least I hope it will be. I really care about her. She's a good person, funny intelligent, beautiful."

"Sounds like she's the whole package."

"And I want you to meet her, you and Jake. I'm going to have a little dinner party at my place, next week Saturday."

She froze. "Next Saturday?"

"Yes, does that work for you?"

"Well, actually . . . I was going to talk to you about next week. I know this is a bad time, but I'm going to have to take a few days off."

"Now, with everything that's going on?"

"Yes, uh, you know my cousin Rita." He nodded. "Well, she's going in for some . . . female surgery. And she's going to need someone to take care of her for a few days when she gets home. We're the only family. She doesn't have anyone else."

His mouth formed a firm line. "Will you be reachable, in case we need you?"

"Of course. You can always get me on my cell phone." She hoped it would work on the ship.

"Hmmm. Well, family is family. How long will you be out?"

"All of next week, for sure. I hope it won't be longer than that." She snatched a glance at her desk clock. Damn, Rita would be walking through the door for their lunch date any second now. "Can you excuse me one minute? I need to check on something with Tara." She hurried out and reached Tara's desk just as Rita stepped off the elevator.

Eva practically ran to Rita. Thankfully, Tara was busy with one of the designers. She grabbed Rita by the arm and turned her back to the elevator.

"Change in plans," she said under her breath. "Don't call the office. I'll call you later." She pushed Rita back on the elevator just before the door closed.

She quickly walked over to Tara. "Uh, Sebastian and I will be busy for a while, so would you hold my calls for me?"

"Sure thing." She looked past Eva. "I swore I saw your cousin just get off the elevator."

"Really?" She laughed. "At first I thought it was her too, and I went rushing over to her like a fool. Just someone who got off on the wrong floor."

Tara looked at her. "Are you sure you're okay? You're acting really frazzled today."

"I do feel a bit warm. Right after I finish up with Sebastian, I think I'll leave early. Try to nip this thing in the bud."

Tara nodded. "Okay."

"Well, let me get back." Eva hurried away, whispering a desperate prayer. *Please let this work.*

"Everything okay?" Sebastian asked when she returned. He scrutinized her with a pinched expression. "I don't see why you didn't just call Tara on the phone. The phones are working, aren't they?"

"Yeah, but I knew she was working with the designers and wouldn't be at her desk."

"Hmmm." He looked at his watch. "Okay, well let's get busy."

"Sure." She was more than happy to sit down. Her legs had gone all wobbly.

Three hours later, they'd finished the preliminary work. They'd matched all the inventory with the in-house files and began the process of seeing what could be cut back.

"There really isn't much room for cuts, Bass," Eva said, rotating her neck.

"Unfortunately, you're right." He pursed his lips in thought. "Our biggest expenses are the rent for this place, salaries, and utilities."

"We can't afford to let any of the designers go, especially not now. And they can't work in the dark."

They both chuckled.

"The only thing we can do, which will save several thousand per month, is to cut back on the hours of operation."

"What? You're kidding!"

He shook his head. "What choice do we have? The staff is going to have to do more in less time. Since they're all paid by the hour, we can cut that way, and if no one is here, that will save on the electric bill, which is astronomical."

"Bass . . . I don't know. . . ."

"If you have a better suggestion, I'd love to hear it."

She had none. "Who's going to tell them? Not me," she added quickly.

The corner of his mouth turned up in a sardonic grin. "Guess that leaves me."

"Yeah, I guess it does."

To say that the staff was disgruntled was a mild understatement, Eva thought as she drove home from work. Sebastian's new work plan was to go into effect the following day, which meant that everyone was in at their same time of eight but would end the day at two. All that might work out in her favor. No one besides her and Sebastian had keys. Once the employees were gone for the day, she could simply come back and remove the boxes. In the morning she'd let Tara know that she was planning on returning them after all.

She turned onto her street. Today's bullets had been dodged, but she was sure there were more where those came from.

12

The next day, Lenora sat next to Stan as she placed the call. It rang on the other end several times before the woman who'd set up her husband answered the phone.

Lenora had gone over every detail of information she'd been able to gather on Suarez and his secret trip into the United States. The shipment wasn't his real agenda, only a small part of it, but it was the only part that interested her. According to everything she'd uncovered, Suarez was coming to the States to settle a personal score with a family member who'd absconded to the U.S. several months ago. That was his business. When she got what she wanted, she'd put in a well-placed call and have Suarez picked up. In the meantime, she had to stay focused.

"I will meet you and your husband at the designated drop-off point in Miami. No fuckups."

"How do we know that this isn't a setup?" Eva asked.

"You don't. But you also have a choice. Do what I tell you to do and walk away, or try to get creative and I can have an agent at your door in five minutes. It's up to you."

"We'll be there."

"That's better. You have the phones that I sent to you?"

"Yes."

"Good. Make sure you have them on at all times. You never know when I may decide to check in. If you don't answer . . ." She chuckled. "Well, we don't want to think about that now, do we?" She paused. "Are we clear about everything?"

"Crystal," Eva said from between her teeth.

"Excellent. Oh, and by the way, you could really stand to lose a few pounds. Your rear end doesn't photograph very well."

Click.

Eva's neck snapped back. "Bitch!" She slammed down the phone just as Jake walked through the door.

"Who?" he asked, hanging his jacket on the coatrack.

"Lenora Ingram," she said, seething with outrage.

"We know that already. What did she do now?"

Eva planted her hands on her hips and rocked from side to side as she spoke. "She indicated that my ass was fat and didn't photograph well."

Jake fought to keep from laughing. He slowly approached. "What does she know about fat asses anyway?" He kissed her cheek and patted her behind. "Probably jealous."

Eva gave him a hard shove.

He snickered. "What did she really want?"

"Wanted to make sure we are going to be where we're supposed to be to make the drop-off."

He crossed the room, plopped down on the couch, and let out a long sigh. "I'll be glad when this is over."

Eva dropped down next to him. "Yeah, so will I. The little bitch is going to get what she deserves."

Jake grinned and draped his arm around her shoulder. "She's going to wish she would have simply paid us the money."

"I know that's right." She turned to Jake. "What time are Rita and Jinx coming tonight?"

"I told them to get here around seven. How'd you make out with the boxes?"

"Believe me, it was touch and go for a minute. I got them out of there today. They're in the bedroom."

"You square everything away with Sebastian?"

"He was pissed that I was going to be out, but I promised him he could always reach me by cell phone in the event of an emergency. But before we leave, I'm going to go over everything I can think of with Tara. She's itching to run the studio one day. This will be her chance, and I'm going to impress that upon her. If I can get her to believe that contacting me is an indication that she isn't ready to handle things"—she bobbed her head up and down—"I won't be expecting any calls."

Jake patted her thigh. "Always on the ball." He pushed up from the couch. "I'm going to take a quick shower and get out of this monkey suit before they get here."

Eva sat there for a few minutes more. Ordinarily she would have been eager to join him in the shower for a quick one, but for some reason she wasn't in the mood. Her nerves were shot, and as much as she'd kept it from Jake, she hadn't been able to sleep soundly since this entire fiasco began.

A part of her resented him for getting them into this mess, and the anger was making her distant. She hated to feel that way, but she did. She couldn't remember a time since they'd met that she hadn't been hot for him twenty-four hours a day. Sooner or later he would notice, if he hadn't already.

She listened to the sound of the shower, tuned in to her body, waited for it to respond to the temptation that was only a few feet away. It never did.

"Did you get approval for the time off from work?" Lenora asked Stan as they stood side by side in the kitchen.

Stan nodded. "It won't be a p-problem."

"Good. I don't want to risk anything by flying down there and having our names on any flight itinerary. So we're going to drive."

"All the way to F-florida?"

She chopped an onion into minuscule pieces with the precision of a samurai warrior. Stan winced at the intensity with which she wielded the knife.

"Yes." She stabbed the knife into the wooden cutting board and turned to him. She wiped her hands on her apron. "It's the best way. It will take two days. We can spend the night in a motel along the way, meet them for the pickup, and then be on our way."

"Lee . . ." His throat worked up and down. "W-what are we going to do a-after this is o-over?"

She looked into his pale blue eyes, hoping to see some remnants of the man she'd married, hoping that her heart would soften. "Don't worry about it. I have everything un-der control." She stroked his hand as she would a pet and went back to preparing dinner.

Stan left Lenora to her work and went into the living room to fix himself a drink. If there was one thing he knew about Lenora, she always had a plan, and his gut told him her plan did not include him. He'd have to have one of his own.

13

"Hold still," Eva warned. "I need to fix this sleeve."

Rita huffed. "Just don't stick me again, okay."

"I wouldn't if you would stay still."

"Hey, Eva, the shirt is missing one of the gold buttons on the shoulder," Jinx called out.

Eva rolled her eyes. They had no clue what it took to put together an entire wardrobe, especially one that had to be mimicked down to the last detail. She went to sleep dreaming about gold buttons and sagging hemlines.

"I swear I don't know what you see in him," Eva said as she made the final adjustment on Rita's sleeve.

Rita chuckled. "The same thing you see in Jake."

"Not possible."

Rita put her hand on Eva's to stop her fingers. "Look, I was never really sure what went down between you and

Jinx. And . . . I don't want to know. But Jinx is a good guy. Give him a break."

Eva sighed. "Maybe. He just rubs me the wrong way."

"That's too bad, 'cause he thinks the world of you and would walk in front of a truck for his brother."

Eva angled her head at her look-alike cousin. She shrugged then lowered her gaze. "I never told anyone this—"

"I know. He made a pass at you. He told me all about it, ages ago."

Eva's head snapped up; her brows rose. "He did?"

Rita nodded. "Jake knows too. You're the only one who thinks it's this big ugly secret."

Eva chortled. "Wow, how dumb have I been?"

"Very. And here's the best part. He thought you were me." She winked.

Eva put her hand on her hip. "You really believe that? You know I'm cuter."

"You wish." Rita grinned. "But seriously, it was a long time ago, cuz. He was a little high." She shrugged. "He would never intentionally go after his brother's woman. You should know that. Jinx isn't that kind of guy."

"Hmmm."

"Listen, we're all going to have to work together on this. Trust each other. You can't let some damned near decade-old bullshit mess with your head."

Eva pouted. She knew Rita was right. It was a long time ago. Jinx had never tried anything since. He always treated her with respect, but she'd thought it was because he believed she would tell Jake. Hmph—she was the last one to know. The joke was on her.

"You're right." She sniffed. "I'll give him a break."

Rita patted her shoulder. "Good girl. Now come on. I want to get out of this thing."

Jake handed Rita, Jinx, and Eva their PDAs.

"Each of them is loaded with the the ship schematics. There's a list of all of the rooms, staff names, and titles. I have the master file on the laptop and can beam information straight to each of the PDAs whenever necessary." He looked at everyone. "Whatever you do, don't lose it. Now let's go over the list one more time. We can't afford to forget anything."

For the next hour they rehearsed their roles, reviewed all the possible scenarios, went over the time schedule and the escape routes.

"The plane leaves for Brazil at six a.m.," Jake continued. He braced his forearms on his thighs and leaned forward. "When we arrive in Brazil, we'll check into a little out-of-the-way motel that Jinx secured, board the ship the following morning, check into our rooms, and then get busy. We have six days before we reach Miami. Six days to put the finger on Suarez, make sure he has what we want, get it, and get out."

"Have you confirmed our transportation out of Miami after the meet?" Eva asked Jinx.

"It'll be taken care of."

"Taken care of! We leave day after tomorrow, Jinx. When do you plan to take care of it?"

"I said I'd handle it, and I will."

Eva jumped up from her seat. "There's a reason why they call you Jinx, John Kelly." She pointed a finger at him. "You better not screw this up."

Jake clasped her wrist. "Relax, Eva," he said softly.

"Relax? How can I relax, Jake, when one wrong blink and we're all going down? Tell me that!"

Eva stormed off in a huff, slamming her bedroom door with such force, the mirror on the dresser shook.

She rubbed her forehead as she paced the bedroom. Why was this freaking her out so? She was a professional. Jake worked out all the details. Everyone was comfortable in their roles. Damnit, she felt like crying. Her eyes burned, and her throat tightened. She sniffed hard.

This was ridiculous. It was like Rita said: they had to trust each other. She just didn't know if she could trust Jinx. Yeah, he'd made a pass at her and he knew perfectly well who she was. But that wasn't the whole of it, and that's what scared her. Jinx had a very bad habit of promising and not delivering. One of his promises landed him in jail, and cost her and Jake fifty thousand dollars.

She and Jake had been working in Arizona. Jinx wanted in on the scam. And Jake, being the "good" brother, agreed. Jinx was the one who was responsible for securing their exit. He swore he had connections with the airlines and could get the packages of heisted goods on board without detection. That never happened, though.

An hour before boarding, he got picked up for using a stolen credit card. The packages remained on the loading dock at the airport with Eva's and Jake's aliases on them.

When they called Jinx on his cell moments before boarding to confirm that everything was a go, but only got his voice mail, they had to nix the whole plan. They drove back to New York from Arizona in a rented car.

Jinx spent three years in jail, and Eva hadn't trusted him since. Everyone seemed to have forgotten that fiasco, but *she* hadn't.

"They're gone. Said to tell you good night."

Eva turned to the door. Jake stood backlit from the living room lamps.

She nodded but said nothing, went to the closet and pretended to look for something.

"Talk to me, Eva. Please."

She lowered her head, fought back a rush of tears. "I don't know what to say, Jake."

"I find that hard to believe. You always have something to say, whether I want to hear it or not."

She smirked in spite of herself. She turned to him. "I've never felt this uneasy about a job. Never. And with Jinx involved . . ."

He clasped her shoulders. "Jinx is going to be fine."

"How can you say that? Every time Jinx is involved, something goes wrong. There was the time in Atlanta with the hotel security. Instead of paying attention to the guard, he was in the lounge with some woman. He was supposed to have an in with tickets for the Astrodome in Houston, said we could make a killing in one night, and the second ticket he scalps was to a cop. Not to mention Arizona."

Jake grimaced, remembering.

"Should I go on? There's a reason he's got that nickname. Baby, this time it isn't the local toy cops or hotel security we're dealing with. This is the FBI. If we go down on this job, we're going away for a very long time."

Jake sat down on the side of the bed. He stretched out his hand toward her. Eva came and sat beside him.

"Have I ever broken a promise to you in all the years you've known me?"

She shook her head.

"I don't intend to now. No matter what happens, we're going to get out of this clean. I swear to you. I've checked and double-checked everything. And believe me, I'm gonna be on Jinx like white on rice. Don't worry. You just concentrate on your part. I'll take care of the rest." He paused, took her chin in his palm, and turned her face toward him. "For better or worse."

She rested her head on his shoulder. "We could do without the 'worse' part."

Jake chuckled. "You got that right." He hugged her close and kissed the top of her head. "Come on, let's get some sleep. I have cars to sell tomorrow, and you have a business to run. It'll be our last night of real sleep for a while."

They made love for the first time in days. It was slow and gentle, as if they were sealing a pact, reaffirming their commitment to each other.

Afterwards, Eva lay curled in Jake's embrace, wishing she could hold on to the moment, but she knew that it was only temporary. Tomorrow wasn't guaranteed.

Jake listened to Eva's deep and regular breathing. She was sound asleep. Gingerly he eased out of the bed and tiptoed out of the room.

He went into the office where the computer was set up. Eva was right. Jinx was a screwup. But in this instance, he wasn't so much worried about Jinx, but about himself.

He turned on the computer and brought up the grid for the security system. There was still one glitch. If he couldn't crack the code for the ship's safe, they were fucked. Plain and simple. He'd beat it; he had to.

Eva turned onto her back and stared up at the ceiling. If Jake was doing what she thought he was, they had more worries than they were prepared to handle. She squeezed her eyes shut and for the first time in more years than she could count, she prayed.

14

JFK Airport was packed, even for five in the morning. Eva and Jake arrived together and went directly to the international check-in. This was the first test.

The counter clerk examined their passports for so long, it made Jake uncomfortable. He traded small talk with Eva as the clerk flipped through the pages, checking his picture against the face on the passport. Finally she handed it back and clicked a few keys on the computer. She gave him his ticket. "Have a safe flight."

"Thanks."

Eva was next, but she wasn't subjected to the same scrutiny.

"One down," Jake said under his breath as they headed toward the second level of security at the departure gate. He put his arm around Eva's waist as they jockeyed around the crowd.

"Have you seen Jinx and Rita?" Eva asked, keeping her focus in front of her.

"They'll be here."

Eva sighed.

"I spoke to him before we left. He'll be here. He was going to pick up Rita on his way."

"We should have all come together."

"No. We don't want to be seen together. We don't want to give anyone cause to make a connection between us."

His cell phone rang just as they approached the security checkpoint.

It was the phone from Lenora Ingram. He flashed Eva a look and then answered the call. "Yeah."

"Your flight leaves in one hour."

"We're going through security now."

"I know."

Jake frowned, took a quick look around.

"Don't bother trying to spot me in the crowd, Mr. Kelly. Be sure not to give them any reason to stop you, and everything will be fine."

He clenched his jaw. "Anything else? We're holding up the line."

"Have a wonderful flight. I'll contact you when you land."

The call was disconnected.

Jake shoved the cell phone back into his pocket. "She's here somewhere."

"Figures. Probably watching us from a camera somewhere."

"We can't worry about her. Just keep our eyes on the prize—that's all." He pulled down two of the plastic bins and began dumping out his jacket pockets: watch, cell phones, and computer into the containers. Eva did the same.

"I still don't see Rita and Jinx," she said, taking off her shoes and adding them to the pile.

"They'll be here."

Jake walked through first without a hitch.

Eva was next. She kept her eyes on her overnight bag. Part of the goods was in her bag, just in case they got separated from their luggage; the rest had been checked through. In case of trouble, she'd printed out the bill of lading at the office and had tucked it away in her purse.

The minute she stepped through the security machine, the lights began to flash.

Shit.

Jake looked back as one of the security guards instructed Eva to turn around and try again. The alarm went off a second time.

"Female officer, please!" the guard shouted in a heavy accent. "Step over to the side, miss."

Eva did as she was instructed, all the while watching the X-ray screen that was examining her bag. The screener signaled for another guard. They both looked, one pointed, the other muttered something she couldn't hear.

"Hold your hands out to your sides, please," a female guard instructed Eva.

She snapped her head in the direction of the voice, praying that they did not decide to open her bag. She held her arms up and to her sides while the guard stroked her body with a hand wand.

"Turn around, please."

Eva did as she was told. The wand slid down the back of her body, hesitating for a moment at her bra strap and then her waist.

"Turn around, please."

Eva drew in a breath and turned around.

"Open the zipper of your pants, please."

"What?"

"Open the zipper of your pants."

"This is ridiculous," she spat as she fiddled with her belt, then the zipper.

The guard moved the wand around the inside of her waistband. "Thank you."

Eva snatched a look at the conveyor belt and breathed a sigh of relief when she saw her bag coming through.

"You're good to go, miss. Sorry for the inconvenience."

"Sure." Eva fixed her clothes.

"Great belt," the guard said.

Eva glanced down at the sparkling belt. "Thanks."

"Where'd you get it?"

"I made it." She grabbed her bag and walked over to Jake. "We should have gone Greyhound," she muttered.

Jake laughed. "You got everything?"

She took a last look around as she adjusted her feet in her shoes. "Yeah. You?"

"Yep. Come on let's go. I need a cup of coffee."

Eva spotted them first. "Well, I'll be damned."

"What?"

She lifted her chin in the direction of the seats at the departure gate. "There's Jinx and Rita."

"See, and you were worried. Two large coffees," he said to the woman behind the counter. Although he wouldn't admit it to Eva, he was pretty relieved.

They took their coffees and walked past Jinx and Rita, taking seats on the other side.

Rita was not her usual flamboyant self, going instead for low-key in her off-white tank top and white denim pants.

She wore a belt almost identical to Eva's but in white. Her auburn wig framed her face in a perfect pageboy cut. Her eyes were shielded behind wide dark sunglasses as if she expected the paparazzi to leap upon her if recognized.

Jinx was just as casual in a pale blue shirt, sleeves rolled halfway up his arms, and a pair of dark jeans. They looked like any other couple traveling on vacation.

Eva had taken out her weave and wore her permed hair in a short spiked look reminiscent of the early Halle Berry cut. Short hair worked much better under the wigs she would have to don during the course of the trip. Jake, always Mr. *GQ*, went about as casual as he allowed: a white shirt without a tie and a navy linen jacket and matching pants.

"Well, all here and accounted for," Jake said, taking a sip of his coffee.

Eva was finally beginning to feel a little better about the whole operation. She had to admit that Jinx surprised her. Not only was he at the airport, but he'd obviously arrived before they did. The knot in her gut began to loosen.

She slid her hand along Jake's thigh. He turned to her, taken aback but delighted. It had been days since Eva had reached for him. Even the other night, it was he who made the overture. He missed the fire, the lust that erupted between them.

"We're gonna be all right, babe," he said only for her ears.

"I think so too." She took his hand. "I know we are going to be on that ship to work—" Her gaze danced over his face. "—but the day has to end sometime."

He ran his tongue along his full bottom lip, but before he could respond, his name was barked out on the intercom system—*his real name*.

Eva and Jake's gazes collided.

"Jake Kelly . . . passenger Jake Kelly, please pick up a white courtesy phone."

"Shit," he spat.

Eva grabbed his wrist. "It has to be her."

"I know," he whispered as he rose from the hard plastic seat. "Be right back."

Eva picked up a newspaper from the seat next to her and feigned interest. She took a glance across the crowded seating space and caught the eye of Rita. Rita shrugged in bewilderment. Eva turned her attention back to the words that were dancing in front of her.

There were several scenarios playing in her head. Either Lenora Ingram was changing the plan, something had gone wrong, or they were screwed before they got started.

She tapped her foot in an uneven rhythm, waiting for Jake to return. Her body tensed when she looked up and saw him approach. His face was unreadable to those who didn't know him, but not to her.

He sat down.

"What happened?"

"It was Stan."

"Stan?"

"Yeah."

"What did he want?"

"A slice of the pie."

15

Stan hung up his office phone. Satisfied. He wiped perspiration from his brow with a white handkerchief, which he then tucked back in his breast pocket. He'd never gone against Lenora. Everything she'd ever wanted he'd done without question, no matter how he felt about it.

He knew what she planned to do. He'd gotten into her computer files at home. *Hmph,* and she thought *he* was a fool. But he had plenty of free time at his job to master the computer and had become quite the hack.

This was his way out, and she wasn't going to deprive him of it. He would get out of his loveless marriage and his dead-end job, and he would start a new life.

That night in the hotel with Leslie, or Eva Kelly, rather, was a blessing in disguise. He knew from the moment he dumped those photos on the coffee table that Lenora would spring into action. All he had to do was play the role of the hapless husband, which he'd gotten down to an art. For the first time in years he saw light at the end of his tunnel, and Lenora was going to get him there.

Lenora stood in front of the team she'd recruited for the Task Force on Border Smuggling, and was issuing their assignments. At first she thought of the detail as yet another albatross around her neck. But maybe she could make it work to her advantage.

"As you all know, Congress is establishing a panel to review smuggling across the U.S. borders. We've been assigned the task of providing the most current information, including names, shipments, and time frames." She looked into the eyes of the three faces: Virginia Holmes, Mike Fuller, and Eric Borden. Eric was a decent-enough fellow; at least he treated her with a degree of respect. Virginia, as much as Lenora disliked her ass-kissing ways, was a whiz with research, and Mike had previous experience on task forces and knew their importance. A motley crew if there ever was one, she thought. But this was what she had to work with. Everyone else in the department was tied up in other projects.

"Virginia, you will handle the research. Go through all our data and pull up everything we have. Mike and Eric, you two work together on any chatter. Then we can compare what you find to what Virginia is able to pull up. Also, Eric check with our people at the Mexican border. Get updates."

They all scribbled furiously. Virginia looked up from her notes.

"And what will you be doing?"

Lenora put her hand on her waist. "Coordinating," she said with a smug look of superiority on her chiseled face.

Mike chuckled and ducked his head.

"Am I missing something?" Eric asked.

"Nothing of importance, I assure you," Lenora said. "If there are no more questions, we can get started. I'll expect daily updates and a full report each week."

They groaned as they got up from their seats. Mike lagged behind after the other two left.

"Yes, Mike? Problem?"

"I just wanted to say that I'm glad to finally be working with you."

Her suspicion alert went to code red. "Why?"

He shuffled the papers in his hands. "As much as I may razz you, I know you're good at what you do."

She wasn't sure how to take it and was waiting for the sexist punch line.

"Anyway, that's all I wanted to say." He turned and left the room.

Lenora stood there for a few minutes, not sure what to make of Mike's admission. She picked up her file folder and tucked it under her arm. Bottom line: she didn't trust anyone. Her goal for the time being was to keep them so busy, they wouldn't have time to pay any attention to what she was doing.

The crew landed in Rio de Janeiro and went to the motel Jinx had scoped out. It was located on the outskirts of the city, in the poorest section. The slums and ghettos of New York had nothing on this place.

Eva cringed when she walked into the shabby lobby of the motel. The heat was unbearable. Flies and mosquitoes apparently ran the joint, and the air reeked of sweat, poor sanitary conditions, old food, and who knew what else. On a hard wooden bench perched precariously against the wall, two derelicts slept.

"You can't be serious about this place?" she whispered to Jake as they approached the front desk.

"I know it's not much, babe, but we need to be as low-key as possible until it's time to board the ship."

She swatted a mosquito away from her neck. "You owe me, Jake, big time," she said from between her teeth.

Rita stepped up to the clerk, who dozed noisily behind the desk.

"Excuse me." She leaned in close, got a whiff of his unwashed body, and quickly stepped back.

In almost slow motion, he opened bleary bloodshot eyes. Sweat ran in a steady stream from his bald head. His shirt was so stained, the original color was lost.

"*Olá.*" He grinned, exhibiting a missing front tooth.

"We need two rooms, *por favor.*"

"*Sim, sim.*" He rolled off his high stool and wobbled over to a row of keys behind him. He took two sets of keys from the hook and handed them to Rita.

"*Obrigada,*" Rita thanked him in Portuguese. She looked at the keys.

"You pay now," he stated more than asked.

Jake stepped up, confirmed the price, and paid him in U.S. dollars. The clerk grinned in snaggletoothed delight.

"Paolo, he take you," he said with a thick accent. "Paolo! Paolo!"

One of the men asleep on the bench stirred.

The clerk shouted something at him in Portuguese. Paolo pulled himself to his feet and shuffled toward them. Rita held out the keys at arm's length. He took the keys without a word and walked outside. Reluctantly the crew followed. Eva punched Jake in the arm.

They followed Paolo across what was once a courtyard and up a flight of weatherbeaten stairs that creaked and groaned under their weight. On the upper level were rows of rooms. Paolo walked halfway down, stopped in front of one, checked the room key, and opened the door.

A cool breeze blew out to greet them. Paolo turned on the light, and a small but immaculately clean room greeted them. A mosquito net hung over a queen-size bed. A ceiling fan whirred silently.

Eva stepped inside and looked around. She walked toward the bathroom and found that to be just as spotless, with relatively modern fixtures, a stack of clean towels, and even those miniature soaps and shampoos they supply at big hotels.

She stepped back out, and Jake was grinning like he'd won something. He pulled their bags inside. He turned to Paolo and handed him five dollars in American money. His eyes brightened, and he muttered his thanks over and over as he backed out the door to take Rita and Jinx to the next room.

"Maybe Jinx isn't such a screwup after all," Eva conceded, sitting down to test out the bed.

"This is one of the hidden treasures. No one with any good intentions or good sense would think twice about stopping here from the look on the outside. If you don't want to be found but still need some creature comforts, this is where you come."

"So I see." She smiled up at her husband and reached for him. He crossed the room, took her hand, and sat beside her. "I'm sorry for being such a bitch lately."

He stroked her hair. "We're all under a lot of strain. It's okay."

"I just want you to know that I'm sorry."

He kissed her lightly on the lips.

"Jake . . ."

"Yeah, baby."

"I need you to tell me the truth."

"Sure."

"Have you figured out the security system for the safe?"

He hesitated. "No." Eva groaned. "Not completely," he continued. "It's titanium with a double switch that's programmed by computer. The code changes daily. That much I have figured out."

She shut her eyes for a moment. "Oh, no. So what are we going to do?"

"If the goods are in the safe, I won't know if I can get in there until the day of."

"Shit," she whispered.

"Exactly." He paused. "Somehow I'm going to have to get access to the ship's computer system, hack in, and find the code."

"Can you?"

"If it comes down to it, I'll get in."

She rested her head on his shoulder. "Thanks for being honest with me. I knew something was wrong."

"Wish I had better news."

"It'll be all right. You're the best." She looked into his eyes. "Right?"

He winked and grinned. "Yeah, I am, ain't I?" He ran his hand down her damp back. "Why don't we try out the shower?" he said, his voice thick with desire.

She smiled, slow and inviting. "Hmmm, I like the sound of that."

"I hoped that's what you'd say." He stood and pulled her to her feet. "Why don't I help you get undressed?" He nibbled her neck.

"One good turn deserves another," she murmured, unfastening his belt.

He pulled her T-shirt over her head. He loved the fact that she rarely wore a bra. The idea that he could simply flash her a look and he could see her nipples harden right in front of him was an exquisite turn-on. He held her breasts in his hands, the fullness of them flowing over his palms. She moaned softly against his ear, her warm breath like butterfly wings against his skin. God, he could never get enough of her. It made him crazy, he thought, pulling her shorts down over her hips. He brushed fingers against her clit. Wet and welcoming, just the way he liked it. He felt her thighs tremble.

They never made it to the shower.

Jake held his wife close, listened to her easy, rhythmic breathing. He stroked her hair. She stirred ever so slightly.

He would do anything for her—just about anything. Eva wanted to get out of the game, settle down. He knew what that meant. She wanted a family.

The thought terrified him. It was the one thing he had to deny her, yet he knew if he did, he'd lose her. Was that a risk he was willing to take?

16

"Got everything?" Jake asked in a pseudo-whisper as they moved toward the ship's gangplank the following morning.

Eva, Rita, and Jinx murmured their assent.

"Once we get on board, we won't be able to meet. The only communication should be via cell or your headset. Any updates will be on your PDAs. I have the cell from Ingram. I'll let you all know when she makes contact."

"What about her husband?" Rita asked as they inched forward.

"We'll deal with him when the time comes. For now, eyes on the prize." Jake handed the crew member his boarding pass.

"You're on the fourth level, sir. Follow the path to your left. Enjoy your trip."

Jake took Eva's hand and helped her on board. She

squeezed his fingers. They looked at each other. "Let's get this party started," Jake said.

"Let's."

With each step they took into the enormous ship, Jake felt unsteady, his legs becoming spaghetti-like beneath him. He tightened his hold on Eva's hand. She turned to him and smiled. His jaw clenched. He could feel perspiration begin to form along his back. They took an escalator to the upper level and followed the corridor around to their cabin.

Jake and Eva had an inside cabin, which was fine with Jake. At least he wouldn't have to look at the misleading calm of the water that would keep them afloat. It was a terror, this phobia he'd never shared with anyone—not with Eva, not with Jinx. He'd never been back to a beach since childhood, since that unforgettable day. He stayed as far away from boats as possible. If there were some other way to pull off this job, he'd do it.

They stepped into their room. He was short of breath.

"Babe, you okay?" Eva asked, staring at him, concern tightening the corners of her eyes. "You're sweating."

An old familiar shudder seized his spine. "I'm fine. Turn on the air," he said, dumping the bag with the laptop on the bed. He unbuttoned a second button on his shirt. "Kinda warm in here."

She gave him a short look then went to the wall panel and turned up the air-conditioning. "Should cool off in a few minutes." She faced him, her head dipped to the side. "You want to tell me what's wrong? Is it the safe?"

He rocked his neck left, right then rolled his shoulders. "Naw, just feel cramped." He focused his gaze on the patterns on the carpet.

The ship shifted ever so slightly. Jake drew in a sharp breath.

Eva reached out, clasped his shoulder. "Baby what's wrong? You look ill, and you're sweating like crazy."

Jake slowly backed away, sucking in air. He reached behind him and felt for the bed, slowly sat down. Eva sat next to him. She felt his forehead.

"You're clammy. Did you eat something?" She thought about the hurried breakfast of eggs and coffee they'd gobbled down at a rest stop. Maybe that was the trouble.

"I'll be all right. Just felt a little weird for a minute." The corners of his mouth flickered into an imitation of a smile.

"Lie down for a few. I'll unpack."

"Yeah, yeah, I think I will." He leaned back against the pillows, threw his left arm across his eyes.

Eva watched him from the other side of the cabin. Jake didn't get sick. He was healthy as a horse. She couldn't remember the last time he'd gotten a simple cold. It was she who usually had to be nursed to health. Her gut told her the sudden symptoms were more psychological than physical. He was afraid—of what, she had no clue. She was pretty sure it wasn't the job. As difficult as manipulating the codes for the safe was, that wasn't something that would make Jake Kelly look as if someone had walked over his grave.

She opened the two carry-on bags they'd brought on board and started to unpack. A gentle knock interrupted her. She peered through the peephole then opened the door.

A young man, a member of the ship's staff, stood with a rolling cart containing the rest of their luggage.

"Thank you. Please bring them right in. You can put them in that corner," she added, pointing to an empty space on the far side of the cabin. She stepped back and let him push the cart into the room. He unloaded the luggage and left.

She glanced at Jake, who still lay supine on the bed as she closed and locked the door. He barely stirred. Concern wrinkled her brow. What wasn't he telling her? If it was something that was going to have an impact on this job, she had a right to know.

She crossed the room and sat next to him. He mumbled something but didn't take his arm from in front of his eyes.

Eva gently shook his shoulder. "Jake. Wake up."

"I'm not asleep."

"Then look at me."

He moved his arm away as if it weighed a ton, letting it flop to his side. He blinked several times to get her in focus. "What's up?"

"That's what I want you to tell me. And don't give me any bullshit about feeling cramped. We've been locked in closer quarters than this, and it never bothered you before. Like the time when we lifted that jewelry and had to hide in the mark's closet for two hours when his son came home."

That ugly incident had turned them forever off of burglary. They'd nearly gotten caught. It was the one time they veered off their regular plan. Instead of their usual picture scam, they'd decided that they would use the information they'd gathered on the mark and lift a few choice items from his house, especially since he couldn't stop telling Eva how much he had and how much he was worth. Breaking in had been a cinch for Jake. But the one thing they didn't count on was the unexpected arrival of the son who'd come home from college two days early. They were stuck in the bedroom closet for two hot, unbearable hours until the son finally went out. They'd barely escaped. Their car actually passed the mark's on their way out on the two-lane road.

During the entire ordeal, Jake was the epitome of cool; he was calm and in control. So this behavior made no sense.

Jake stared up at the ceiling.

"Is whatever it is that's happening with you going to affect this job?"

He turned his head to look at her. "No."

Eva pressed her palm against his chest. "This is me, Jake. Whatever it is, you can tell me."

He looked away. "It was a long time ago," he murmured.

"What was?"

He squeezed his eyes shut for a moment. "I was around nine. Me and Jinx and Earl."

Eva tried to recall someone named Earl. She couldn't. Jake never mentioned anyone named Earl.

"One minute we were playing tag on the shoreline and the next . . ." He sighed heavily, ran his tongue across his lips.

"What happened?"

"He was just gone. Disappeared, right in front of our eyes as if he never existed. The water took him."

Eva put together the jagged pieces of the puzzle. Jake had watched his childhood friend Earl get sucked away by a wave, probably a riptide. No wonder he never wanted to go swimming or sailing.

"I never got over it, not really. Had nightmares for years. Thought I'd pretty much gotten it out of my system . . . until we got on the ship." In his child's mind, he'd connected water with loss, having the ability to engulf someone you cared about and take them away forever. And that connection had lain dormant—until today.

"Jake," she said as gentle as she could. "Why didn't you ever tell me?"

He shook his head. "Ego thing, I guess."

"Ego?"

"Didn't want you to see me weak or afraid." He sputtered a laugh.

"I would have seen you as a human being who experienced a traumatic event. We all have stuff that messes with our head."

He challenged her with a hard look. "What messes with your head, Eva?"

She thought for a moment. She wanted to be honest. "I have a constant fear that I'll lose everything, including you."

He turned on his side and propped himself up on his elbow. "Why?" he asked, his voice rising an octave.

"You know some of my life growing up." She looked at him. He nodded for her to go on. "When my mother walked out on me and me never knowing my father, then Rita's mom dying on us and my grandmother not wanting to be bothered with either of us left me feeling like you can't put your feelings into anyone, because if you do, they can be taken away or, worse, not share those same feelings for you." She looked at him.

The sadness he saw in her twisted his stomach with a pain that he very well understood. He sat up, gathered her close. "You'll never lose me, Eva," he breathed into her ear. "Never. I swear that to you."

She held on for a moment before easing back. "How can I ever be sure?" Her dark eyes danced over his face, searching for the truth.

"There are no guarantees in life, but as long as I have a breath in my body and the ability to do so, I'll be with you." He stroked her cheek. "I've never broken a promise to you. Never."

She lowered her head. "Guess we're two pretty messed-up individuals, huh?"

"More like kindred spirits." A half smile softened the lines of his face. He tucked his finger beneath her chin and lifted her head. "Let's make a deal."

She twisted her lips to the side, eyeing him with suspicion. "What kind of deal?"

"You keep me from flipping out on this ship, and I promise to make sure that you're never alone. How's that?"

When she grinned, the corners of her eyes crinkled. "I like the sound of that."

"Good. I have to be honest."

"What?"

"This safe thing is bugging me. But I'm going to nail it. I need to play around with the encryption program some more. I'm close—I can feel it."

"You'll pull it off. You always do."

He pushed up from the bed.

A blast from the ship's horn signaled their departure.

They looked at each other.

"No turning back now," Eva said.

"Not a chance. Let's get to work."

"I'll call Jinx and Rita. Is an hour enough time?"

Jake nodded. "We should be well under way by then."

Eva pulled the toss-away cell phone from her purse and dialed Rita's room. "Be ready for the first round in an hour."

17

The quartet met at the entrance to the casino. They hadn't been out to sea more than a couple of hours, and already the blackjack and roulette tables, and the one-armed bandits, were experiencing heavy traffic. The sights and sounds were similar to those of any of the major casinos in Atlantic City or Vegas. Lights flashed, money changed hands, and laughter and drinks flowed.

Jake, Jinx, and Eva were dressed in their crew-member attire: white button-up shirt, with the ship's insignia on the sleeve, black vests, and matching slacks. Rita was the hook. She wore white, a deep V in the front of her summer dress exposing just enough cleavage to be tempting to the eye. Her shoulder-length auburn weave was pulled away from her face and neck and held on top of her head with a gold barrette.

They each had the standard headsets for communication among employees, except that theirs ran on a separate signal. Rita's was a single earpiece with a high-powered microphone, courtesy of Jinx.

"Remember," Jake said before they separated, "blend in and look busy."

Jake took the casino floor, Eva went to the upper deck, Jinx took the lounge, and Rita combed the sky pool, all with the intention of getting a lay of the land, identify any potential problems, and of course, to spot Xavier Suarez.

For the next few hours they rotated floors, covering all fourteen levels.

"What if he's not here?" Jinx spoke into his headset from the Promenade Deck. He walked across the deck, stepping around the waves of passengers heading to the game rooms.

"Hey, if he ain't, I'm gonna have the time of my life on this ship," Rita responded from the bar. She caught the eye of a man who looked a heck of a lot like Don Johnson in his youth. He winked. She winked in return.

"He just walked in," Jake hissed into his microphone.

"Where are you?" Eva asked, looking around from her station near the spa. She pressed her finger to her earpiece.

"Panorama Deck." He glanced at the numbers embossed on the pillar. "Level ten. Rita, make your way up here."

"Excuse me. Can you tell me where the sauna is?" a lithe female draped in a flimsy gauze wrap and a two-piece bikini asked Jake.

Jake blinked, for a moment forgetting that he wore the crew uniform. "Oh, sure, um, it's on the sixth level. You can take the escalator to your left or the elevator a little farther down the hall." All that studying of the layout was paying off early.

Her blue eyes rolled hungrily over him. "Thank you. Um." She put a red-tipped nail to her lips. "What time do you get off? Maybe we can have a drink together later."

"Who the hell is that?" Eva blasted into his headset.

Jake winced. "Sorry, miss. It's against policy." He smiled apologetically.

She pouted. "That's too bad." She ran her tongue across her lips then walked off.

"Jake! Jake Kelly!" Eva barked, knowing full well that he was giving her that charming smile of his.

"Would you relax? It was a passenger asking for directions." He chuckled to himself.

"She was asking for a lot more than directions." Eva rolled her eyes as she trotted up a flight of stairs, turned left down a long, busy corridor then toward the escalator.

"Play nice, children," Jinx said, making his way to the tenth level.

Rita arrived first. She spotted Jake, who walked in the direction of Suarez. Jake tipped his head slightly to the right to point Suarez out to Rita as he passed. Suarez took a seat at the bar. Two men flanked him.

Rita gave an imperceptible nod. Took her earpiece out and stuck it in her bag. Her eyes roamed the room. Jinx entered from the far right. Eva came up on the elevator.

"He's the one in the white shirt with the two bulldogs on either side of him," Jake said into his headset for Jinx and Eva's benefit.

Rita surveyed the passengers. Checked out the two bartenders. She opted for the seat on the opposite side of the round bar. Suarez would have no choice but to notice her. She ordered a Scotch on the rocks, took out a pack of cigarettes from her purse. She reached for a book of matches in the circular ashtray on the bar counter. Lit her cigarette and blew a long plume of smoke into the air.

Her drink arrived.

As she raised the glass to her lips, she looked over the rim and directly into the eyes of Xavier Suarez. Her "G"-spot hit a high note. He was gorgeous. The blurry pictures that Jake had of him were a disservice.

His skin was the color of burnished bronze, and his face was chiseled. Dark soulful eyes, almost black with thick sweeping lashes that looked as if they'd been painted on with an artist's brush. His mouth was lush, his bottom lip full, the top kissed by a thin inky black mustache. The thick head of hair was raven black as well and combed back from the wide forehead. Raw, sexual energy radiated from him in waves.

Suarez took a cigar from the breast pocket of his snow-white shirt and cut off the tip with a deadly-looking object. The man to his right quickly took out a lighter and lit the cigar. Suarez barely acknowledged him. The bartender set a bottle of brandy in front of them and filled three glasses before returning his attention to the other customers at the bar.

The man on his left leaned close to Suarez, whispered something in his ear. Suarez pursed his lips and then slid his eyes in Rita's direction. She boldly stared back at him, leaned a bit forward to flick ashes in the ashtray and give him a momentary peek at her cleavage.

Rita watched his lips move but couldn't make out what he was saying. She sipped her drink. The man to his right signaled a passing waiter. Moments later, the three men rose and walked out into the adjacent dining room, Suarez leading the way.

"Elvis has left the building," Rita murmured after replacing her earpiece under the guise of fixing her earring.

"He's being seated at a banquette in the dining room," Eva said, walking into the elegant room. She picked up a discarded tray from the cart and walked around, recovering used glasses from the table. "All the way in the back," she whispered.

"Notice any other players?" Jake asked, surveying the space as best he could, hoping to spot any likely bodyguards. He slowly walked toward the bar, around the tables with his hands tucked behind his back as if overseeing the activities.

"There's a guy standing near the elevators. Been there for a while," Jinx said. "Short, kinda stocky. Dark suit, no tie."

Jake retraced his steps and headed for the elevator. When he was in front of it, he pressed the button, checked his watch, frowned, shook his watch. "Do you have the time? I hope my shift will be over soon." He flashed an affable smile.

The man's eyes narrowed as if clicking a mental picture of Jake. "No," he responded with a thick accent.

"Thanks, anyway. Enjoy your cruise." He stabbed the button again, glanced up at the numbers, then hurried off.

"He's definitely one of them," Jake said, walking toward the escalators. "That makes at least three that we have to concern ourselves with. I'm going back to the room. The ship's passenger list should be accessible now. Gonna find out what room Suarez is in. When I do, I want Eva to go by there and see if we have anyone guarding the front door."

Jake returned to his cabin and flipped open the laptop. He loaded the spy program he'd perfected and began searching for the ship's manifest. Within moments, the entire list of more than two thousand passenger names appeared along with their room assignments. He grinned. "Technology."

He scrolled the list and after several moments realized that Suarez's name was not on it. Concern carved several lines in his forehead. He searched the list again, thinking he may have missed it. He didn't.

"Damnit."

He put on his headset. "Suarez's name is not on the list," he said into the microphone. "He must have registered under another name."

"What should we do?" Jinx asked.

"Rita, is he still in the restaurant?" Jake asked.

"Yes, they're being served now."

Jake thought for a moment. "Okay, listen. Get yourself a table in the general vicinity if you can. Keep an eye on him. If they leave, let Eva know, and Eva, you find a way to follow them without being obvious. Jinx, keep an eye on the guy by the elevator. Chances are when Suarez is ready to leave, they'll all leave together."

"And what are you going to be doing, sweetheart?" Eva cooed.

"Going to get friendly with the security team near the safe."

"Be careful."

"I will. I'll use my charm."

"Then we're really up shit creek," Rita teased.

"Very funny. Get busy, everyone."

Jake signed off and then went back to the computer. He pulled up the ship's diagrams. The security office was on the lower deck. It was the hub of the ship. The room was constantly manned by no fewer than four technicians. Their job was to ensure that the security system was operational at all times, from credit card processing to door entries to monitoring the cameras in the casinos and changing the access codes daily. The ship safe was on the fifth level, directly behind customer service. Jake had yet to figure out how he would get into the safe if indeed that's where Suarez was keeping the stash. He'd pretty much figured that the process for changing the codes followed a sequence. He'd almost narrowed it down. From what he'd been able to determine, not only was the code changed daily, but twice per day—once in the morning at eleven and then again at eight. What he had to do was nail down the pattern. He was close. He could feel it. His fingertips tingled and his dick vibrated. Everything hinged on him getting it right, and he *would* get it right. He had no intention of explaining to Eva from behind bars how he'd screwed up. Or worse.

A cell phone rang.

He looked at the two phones on the bed. It was the phone from Lenora Ingram.

He breathed deep, picked it up.

"Yes," he said the word in a serpent's hiss.

"There's been a change of plans," Lenora said. "You're going to meet me in Mexico instead of Miami."

Jake briefly shut his eyes as he listened and knew they were screwed for real.

18

Eva made herself look busy as she moved around the myriad travelers, keeping a surreptitious eye on the mark. What concerned her even more than keeping Suarez on the radar was the look of hunger that hovered in Rita's eyes every time her glance slid in Suarez's direction. She'd seen that look before. Many times. Rita's lust, when unchecked, could be detrimental to everyone. She'd lose focus on the job and allow herself to become distracted by her libido.

Eva understood. Both of them desperately sought something, something that would allow them to feel worthwhile and whole. She'd been lucky. She'd found Jake. He filled the abyss in her soul. Rita remained on the quest.

Eva had begun to think that as much as she didn't particularly care for Jinx as "the one" for her cousin, that maybe Rita saw something in him that she absolutely couldn't.

She watched Rita lick her lips while her eyes grew dark. No doubt, Suarez *was* a gorgeous man. But they were there to do a job.

Eva made her way over to Rita. She turned off her headset so that her end of the conversation wouldn't reach Jake and Jinx.

"Good afternoon," Eva said. "Enjoying your trip so far?"

Rita turned her attention to Eva. She smiled.

"Yes, I am."

"Remember why we're here," she said quietly as she leaned forward and put two empty glasses on her tray.

"I do," Rita said in a faraway voice.

"Rita," Eva said. "It's a job. Nothing more."

Rita's gaze snapped in Eva's direction. She lifted her glass to her lips, finished off her drink. "I know that."

Eva gave a short nod and walked off.

Since they were little girls with no real family to speak of and no male figure in their lives, they'd been joined at the hip, not only as cousins but also as kindred spirits, seeking validation for their existence. They learned early that being attractive females was more than an asset. It was power. They learned to wield it from a simple smile to mindblowing sexual escapades. They used whatever was necessary to achieve their ends and to smother the fires of need.

For Eva the fire was physical. As long as she could satisfy her physical desires through sex, she felt as if she could face the next day. She was turned on as much by the job as by the act itself.

Rita's need was as much physical as it was emotional. She never could separate the two. She saw her unknown father in every man she met and sought his love and approval. Her physical lust often morphed into an emotional attachment—that was not only dangerous, but stupid as well. There was no room for stupidity on this trip. One of her flights of fancy nearly got her killed.

About two years earlier, Eva and Rita decided on an overdue vacation, leaving men, work, and troubles behind. As much as Jake poked his lip out about her leaving him for a whole week, he agreed that the time away would do her good. He assured her that he'd stay out of trouble in her absence and that maybe she'd be able to show him some new Caribbean moves upon her return.

They booked one of those quick getaways online and landed in Montego Bay in Jamaica. The lush scenery, tropical breeze, and gorgeous men made the brochure and Web site pictures look like pure misrepresentations.

"We should have done this a long time ago," Rita had breathed in wonder when they stepped out of the airport terminal to be met by row after row of men who seemed to want no more than to make a woman happy. She draped her straw bag over her shoulder, slipped on her dark shades to dim the blinding sunlight, and sashayed over to an Adonis of a man who posed casually against the side of a taxi.

Eva trailed two steps behind her.

"Maybe you can help me," Rita said, looking up into his eyes. "My cousin and I need a ride to our hotel."

Briefly he glanced past Rita to take in Eva. He smiled, all dazzling white and even against skin that was as smooth as milk chocolate and dark as midnight. The white gauze shirt was open almost to the waist, revealing thick chest muscles and rippling abs. His hair reached the middle of his back, the lustrous dark locks held in place by a leather tie at the nape of his neck.

"A man's duty is to make a woman's life easier," he said, his accent like music, his voice a gentle rumble.

Even Eva had to admit to herself that he was one gorgeous specimen.

"I can take you anywhere you want to go. This island is a part of me, and there is no place on it that I do not know . . . intimately."

Eva could almost *hear* Rita's heart pumping in her chest.

They got into his cab and soon learned that his name was Jon. He'd been born and raised on the island and made his living as an artist and cabbie. He invited them to "see his etchings" at his bungalow later that evening. He was expecting friends over for a show of his new works.

Of course Rita agreed.

When they arrived at his opening, Rita became quickly swept up in his charms and instead of spending the night in their hotel, Rita spent the night with Jon.

Their hot and heavy fling flourished in the ensuing days, with them spending all their time together. On the surface it seemed harmless enough, and Eva kept herself occupied with shopping and sightseeing. But things took an ugly turn shortly before she and Rita were scheduled to depart for the States.

"He wants to come back to New York with us," Rita said over breakfast at an outdoor café.

The forkful of mango that Eva lifted to her mouth stopped midway. "What?"

"He wants to come back to New York, stay with me for a while, see how he likes it."

"You told him no, didn't you?"

Rita looked sheepish, a sly smile curving her lush mouth. "No."

The fork dropped to the plate. "Rita, you don't know this man. How can you even think of having him come and live with you?" She looked around, realizing her voice had risen in alarm, and she hoped no one else noticed. Apparently the softly playing steel drums muffled her concern.

Rita pursed her lips. "I do know him. He's wonderful, and he makes me feel wonderful."

"Don't be ridiculous. Just because the sex is good is no reason to think you actually have a relationship. You can't be serious."

"I already got his ticket."

"Have you lost what's left of your mind?"

"Did I say that to you when you met Jake?"

Eva blinked several times. Yes, her and Jake's initial meeting was over the top, but that was different, and she told Rita as much.

"Why is it different, because it's you? Since when did you have a lock on making a relationship work? You have some kind of psychic ability that I don't know about?"

"It doesn't take a psychic to tell you that you don't move a total stranger into your house." She paused when she saw the stern look of determination light Rita's eyes. When she got that look, the more you pushed, the deeper she dug in her heels.

Eva took a breath, eased back. "Hey, you're a grown woman. If that's what you want to do, you're right: Who am I to say different? Maybe he's the one." She shrugged her sleeveless shoulders.

"He is, Eva," she said with the childish joy of a love-drunk teenager. "You'll see."

And they did.

Two nights before they were scheduled to leave, Jon apparently asked for money, said he needed it to take care of some business before they left. Rita balked, said she'd spent all her extra money on his ticket and that her credit card was at its limit. That didn't sit too well with him, and his gentle cajoling turned belligerent—then violent.

It was about three a.m. when Eva heard a faint knock on their hotel door. When she went to answer it, Rita literally fell into the room. He'd beaten her unconscious, taken the cash she had left in her purse, and dropped her body on the beach. When she'd come to, her clothes tattered and her purse gone, she'd somehow been able to make it back to the hotel.

Her beautiful face was a mass of dark bruises. Both her eyes were swollen, her lip was busted, and they didn't learn until they'd gotten home that one of her ribs was cracked.

Eva wanted to call the police. Rita begged her not to, saying it would only make things worse. He had friends. Eva didn't even want to know what that meant. Besides, Rita added, if they reported it to the police, they'd be forced to stay in Jamaica a few days at least, and all she wanted to do was go home.

Stomping down on her temper, thinking through the ramifications, Eva finally agreed not to call the police.

After tending to Rita's bruises and getting her settled in a hot bath, she contacted the airport, rearranged their flight, and had them on the earliest plane back to New York.

They never spoke about Jon and Jamaica ever again. Rita stayed closeted away in her apartment until her bruises healed. No one was the wiser. And the lie she told her doctor about falling down the stairs accounted for her cracked rib. It was a secret that they kept between themselves and left behind in Montego Bay.

That same look in Rita's eyes that was there for Jon had come back, for Xavier Suarez, this time. Jon was nothing compared to Suarez. If what they said about Suarez killing

his own sister was true, he wouldn't think twice about doing the same to Rita if he found out that she'd set him up or
crossed him in any way.

Rita needed to start thinking straight, and in a hurry.

Eva emptied an overflowing ashtray as she continued to
survey the room and its occupants. All the reminiscing
about steamy Jamaica had her a bit worked up. She put her
tray down on one of the many serving tables and headed
back to her cabin.

Maybe Jake was up for a little romp to christen their
quarters.

"Rita, I'm going up to the cabin for a few. Any changes,
let me know."

"Sure."

She knew she was supposed to stay on post, just in case
and especially knowing what she did about Rita. The excitement of the hunt was getting to her, building like a slow
boil, and she couldn't help herself.

But when she returned to the cabin and saw the look on
Jake's face, she knew her plans would have to wait.

She shut the door.

"What is it?"

"Ingram just called."

"And?"

"She wants to change the drop-off location."

"What! She can't do that. It'll screw up everything." She
crossed the room to the small bar, took a glass, and fixed a
quick drink of rum and Coke. She turned to Jake. "What are
we going to do?"

"We don't have too much choice."

"So if not Miami, then where?"

"The ship is scheduled to dock in Mexico for a day. That's where she wants to make the exchange."

"That cuts our time down by two days." She took a swallow of her drink and sat down in the chair near the bar. Immediately she got back up and started to pace, the reason for her impromptu return to the cabin pushed aside. "How are you making out with the codes?"

Jake was morose. "Close but no cigar." He looked up at Eva.

She tugged on her bottom lip with her teeth. "And we still don't know what room Suarez is in."

The ship began a gentle rocking that grew more violent as the waves picked up.

Color drained from Jake's warm brown complexion, giving him an ashen look. His eyes became glassy.

Eva approached slowly and sat next to him. "Babe. It's cool. We probably hit some bad weather." She rubbed his back.

Jake licked his dry lips and fought to keep from throwing up. He kept seeing waves and then nothing.

The ship lurched to the left then right.

Jake clenched his teeth. Sweat beaded across his brow and upper lip.

Eva stroked his cheek and then wiped the sweat away from his forehead with the pad of her thumb.

"Try to relax. I'm sure it will pass soon."

Jake lay back against the pillows and closed his eyes. He'd never wanted anyone to see him like this, especially not his wife, especially not now. He couldn't afford to fall apart. So much of the plan hinged on him. He had to get a grip.

"It was a freak accident, Jake," Eva said softly. "There was nothing you could have done. It wasn't your fault."

"But it was."

Eva flinched. "Of course it wasn't. You all were just playing by the water. It was an accident."

Jake slowly shook his head. "Me and Jinx . . . we dared him. Dared him to go farther out. He was afraid. We told him he was just being a baby."

The ship rocked a bit then settled.

"He didn't want to do it." His voice cracked. "But we kept taunting and teasing him. He was crying, but he went. And then he . . . was gone." He swallowed hard. "We never told anyone what really happened. Never."

Eva squeezed his hand. "You were kids. How could you have known? You couldn't."

"I can still see the look of shock and grief on his mother's face." He squeezed his eyes shut, the images of that day racing through his mind.

"Jake . . . part of your guilt has been holding on to this secret all these years. It's not a secret anymore. You've finally faced the demon that's been haunting you by sharing it with me. You can get through this. But you have to let it go. Nothing you will ever do can bring him back. You must accept that and accept the fact that it was an accident."

Jake looked at Eva, letting her words sink in. His soul did feel a bit lighter. The weight that he'd been carrying around for so long was not so heavy anymore. He shared the burden, and she accepted it without recriminations. She didn't see him as weak or evil.

His words emerged slowly, coming together in bits and pieces. "For years I'd been living on the edge, a part of me wanting to get caught, as if by doing so, I could pay for what I'd done. I've spent my whole life taking things from others, unsuspecting victims, repeating what I'd started years earlier on that beach, hoping to get caught, hoping to pay."

He sat up, as realization struck him. "Lenora Ingram is

no unsuspecting victim. She's no innocent bystander who doesn't know any better that could be manipulated into doing what we wanted. She was the one who for the first time turned the tables on me." The right corner of his mouth jerked upward. "Forced me to face my fears, unwittingly, but she'd done it. Underneath it all, that's what scared me the most, Eva, that I'd be the unsuspecting victim, and wouldn't hold the winning hand." He paused, looked Eva in her eyes. "But I do." He tapped the side of his head with his index finger. "It's all up here."

She leaned forward and kissed him. "I was waiting for you to say that."

He grinned then pulled her down on top of him. "That's why I love you," he said, brushing his lips against hers.

"Oh, really."

"Yeah, really." He frowned for a minute. "Now that I think about it, what are you doing here? I thought you were supposed to be keeping an eye on things in case Suarez and his boys headed back to their cabin."

Her grin held a hint of mystery. "Well . . . while I was standing there thinking about everything at stake, the pieces coming together and all . . ." She began unbuttoning his shirt. "I started thinking . . . got a little warm all over." She ran her hands across his bare chest. "And I realized . . ." She leaned down and ran her tongue across his nipple.

"What did you realize, baby?" he asked, his voice growing thick. He pulled the black wig from her head and tossed it on the floor.

"I realized how badly I wanted you." She worked at unfastening his belt.

"How bad?" He pulled her vest off and unbuttoned her blouse. His palms cupped her breasts.

Eva moaned, her lids fluttered closed. She ground her hips against his hard-on.

Jake flipped her onto her back, unfastened her pants, and pulled them down. He didn't bother with her thong, merely pushed it aside and slid into her heat.

The gentle sway of the ship only intensified their own push and pull, and Jake let go of his fears for the first time in his life, letting Eva's loving wash them away.

"I better get back," Eva murmured in a dreamy voice.

Jake held her close. "Yeah," he said without much conviction. He draped one leg over her body.

"You're making that kind of difficult." She giggled.

"Oh, am I?" he asked, feigning innocence.

"Yes." She pushed against his chest, and he fell back onto the bed. She sat up and looked down at him. His eyes were closed, and he smiled softly. "You have work to do, and so do I."

"I thought I was working, and doing a damn good job, by the sound of things." He chuckled and opened his eyes. "But you're right." He pushed himself halfway up. "We need to get busy."

Eva got up off the bed, stretched, gathered her clothes, and walked toward the bathroom. "Gonna take a quick shower." She closed the door behind her.

Jake yawned loudly just as Jinx's voice came through the headset. "He's on the move."

Jake put the set on. "Keep an eye on him until Eva gets there."

"Where the hell is she?"

"Taking a shower," he said, the simple words full of innuendo.

"Hope it was inspiring."

"Always is. She'll be there shortly."

Eva came out of the bathroom, the towel wrapped around her body.

"Jinx just chimed in. Suarez is on the move. Hopefully, he's headed back to his cabin. Jinx will keep an eye on him."

Eva dressed as she listened. "I'm pretty sure a man like Suarez is in one of the suites." She buttoned her blouse.

Jake nodded. "And his bodyguards are going to be close by."

She put on her pants and vest. "We'll take care of our end; you finish up on the codes."

"That's the plan."

She crossed the room, leaned down, and kissed him lightly. "I love you, Jake Kelly."

"Back at ya."

She grinned and then headed out.

Jake went immediately back to his computer. The software that he'd installed was running a sequence program against the ship's security system. The probabilities were being narrowed down. When he checked again, the sequence was finished, the final screen was flashing EXECUTION COMPLETED.

Jake hooked up the computer to the portable printer and printed out the results. As he read over the report, his smile grew. "Houston, we no longer have a problem."

19

"Where is he?" Eva asked as she walked the corridors back to the restaurant.

"We're getting on the elevator going up. I'm turning off my set," Jinx said as he boarded the elevator.

Eva arrived back at the restaurant. Rita was nowhere to be seen. Eva's heart jumped. She looked around. "Rita I'm at the bar. Where are you?"

Several moments passed with no response.

"Rita, can you hear me?"

"I was getting bored and was beginning to look suspicious sitting at the bar. When I saw him leave, I went in the opposite direction. I'm in the casino near the roulette table."

Eva's heart began to slow to its normal rhythm. "Okay. I'm waiting to hear from Jinx."

"What's going on with Jake?"

"He's working. Listen, stay put. I'm coming to you."

Eva wound her way around the passengers en route to the casino. It was apparent that after all the travelers were fully settled in their cabins, they were hell-bent on seeing the sights of the ship. People were everywhere. Some towns didn't have as many people as this ship. The casino was packed. It took Eva a while to find Rita.

"Everything cool?" Eva asked, standing to her cousin's right.

"Sure."

"You had me worried."

"Don't."

Eva moved around the throng of observers as the die-hard gamblers and those who felt lucky played at the table.

Jinx's voice popped in her ear. "He's on the eleventh level. Room 1176. He has an outside cabin."

Eva turned her back to the table, looked out into the crowd. "Did they go in with him?"

"Yeah, all three of them. Wait. Two of them just came out. Going down the hall. They went into room 1170."

"Thanks, Jinx. That leaves one with our man. Meet me at the base. I'll get Rita."

Eva walked past Rita and murmured for her to come back to base. Rita waited a reasonable amount of time and headed to Jake and Eva's cabin.

"Okay, so we know they're using at least two cabins," Jake began once everyone was settled. He brought up the schematics of the eleventh level on the television screen that he'd hooked up to the computer.

"More than likely, one of his men is staying in the room with him," Eva said.

"If that's the case, it may be because the stash is in his room," Rita offered.

"Could be. Somehow we have to get into that room before we dock in Mexico."

"Why Mexico?" Jinx asked.

Jake brought them up to speed.

Jinx let out a stream of expletives. "That fucks up everything. I have stuff set for Miami. Everything."

"I know, I know," Jake said. "You're gonna have to work your contacts. Let them know there's been a change in plans and location. Everything is going to have to be moved and in place in the next couple of days."

"Shit!" Jinx paced the room.

Rita asked the question that was on all of their minds. "What if Ms. Girl changes locations again?"

"She wants to ensure that we don't have enough time to screw her," Eva said.

"Exactly. So we need a plan C," Jake said.

"Which is?" Jinx asked.

"That's what we're going to sit here and figure out. The one thing on our side is that there are only so many stops. She has to know that we need time to pull it off. It can only be Mexico or the final stop in Miami."

Jinx snapped his fingers. "I can find out exactly where she's going to be."

"How?" Rita asked.

"All the agents have to be reachable. If she's leaving town, she's going to have to log it in."

Jake nodded, seeing where Jinx was going with his train of thought.

"I'll tap into the FBI files, see what I can dig up."

"And what about the husband?" Eva asked. "He's another thorn in our side."

"Yeah, he said he wanted in," Rita said. "So what do we do about him?"

"Let his wife worry about him. I'm pretty sure that he'll be with her if he wants his end," Jake said. "In the meantime, Jinx, you get busy with the FBI files. Rita, get ready for this evening. Knowing what I know about Suarez, he's a hard gambler. He'll be in the casino."

Rita nodded.

"Eva, you keep an eye on the rooms, let us know the comings and goings. The minute it's empty, let me know."

"What are you planning?" Eva asked.

"When they come out, I'm going in."

Rita returned to the cabin she shared with Jinx to prepare for the evening ahead.

Jinx came in behind her, closed and locked the door.

"Things are kinda sticky," he said, pulling off his vest.

"Hmmm."

He glanced at her. "You okay?"

"Fine."

Jinx crossed the room, sat down on the chair, then took off his shoes.

"Something on your mind, Rita?"

She turned, looked at him for a moment. How could she tell him that she was having wild fantasies about Xavier Suarez, that looking just once into his eyes had stirred up the beast in her, clouded her thoughts? Of course she couldn't.

"Just everything, I guess," she finally said. "So much could go wrong." *You have no idea.*

Jinx got up to stand in front of her. He pushed a stray lock of hair away from her cheek. "It's gonna be cool. We're gonna be rich, and then . . . me and you are gonna live large." He grinned, that same devilish grin his older brother had perfected.

She forced a smile. "I know you're right." She kissed him lightly on the lips. "I better shower and change." She turned away and went into the bath.

Moments later, Jinx heard the rush of water. He sighed heavily. How long had he carried a thing around in his heart for Rita? He knew the kind of woman she was. She was a chameleon, changing at will. Not only her appearance, but her emotions as well.

Some days he honestly believed that he was the one who could settle her down. Other days he didn't know who she was. He'd see that faraway look in her eyes, like she was staring right through him. It was the look she had now—as if he didn't really matter, as if he were just another mark.

He'd been around when Rita had taken many of her romantic spills. He'd been the one to pick her up and put the pieces back together again. Like that time she and Eva went to Jamaica. He didn't know what actually happened; they never said. But he knew it was bad. She'd stayed away from him for weeks after her return. And when she resurfaced, she offered no explanation. She was quiet and reserved, often crying in her sleep. But he'd stayed, told her that whatever it was they'd get through it together.

Then one day she was the old Rita again, full of fun and laughter, looking for her next adventure.

The shower water cut off. When she stepped out of the bathroom, barely noticing him, his bad feeling only intensified. And his gut told him it had to do with Xavier Suarez.

Rita dressed in silence while Jinx worked on getting into the FBI daily logs. Periodically he glanced her way, hoping to catch a glimpse of what was going on in her head. But if there was one thing he knew about Rita, it was that you couldn't push her.

She turned, putting the diamond stud in her ear. "I'll see you later. I'm going to head up to the casino. See what I can see." She picked up her beaded purse from the top of the dresser.

"Sure. I'll be up soon." He looked at her for a moment. Rita was a stunning woman by anyone's standards. Both she and Eva were close ringers for the young actress Dorothy Dandridge, from physical makeup to their finely angled features and cool brown complexions. They could make any man crazy. "Are we okay?" he asked.

She looked down, opened her purse, fishing for her cigarettes. "Of course." She didn't meet his eyes when she replied. She snapped her purse shut, blew him a perfunctory kiss, and walked out.

Jinx slowly shook his head before turning his attention back to the computer. Yeah, she could make a man crazy, all right.

Rita stepped off the elevator, emerging on the casino floor. She took in the swelling crowd, the glitter, the noise, the flashing lights. A rush of energy heated her insides. She felt lucky and went straight to the blackjack table. No one said she couldn't enjoy herself.

She found a seat and was dealt in the next hand. Blackjack was her game; she knew how to call and bluff with the best of them. But what was most important, she knew how to count cards.

She won the first hand, the second, the third, the fourth.

Her winnings piled up in front of her, and she felt unstoppable. A crowd grew behind her, cheering her on.

Eva noticed the commotion and made her way to where the crowd had gathered. As she squeezed her way in between bodies, her heart jerked in her chest when she saw that all the attention was focused on Rita.

She muttered a curse under her breath. There was no way to get her out of there without causing more attention. This was not what they were supposed to do. Attracting attention, sticking out in the crowd was not the plan. *Damnit, Rita.*

Eva spotted movement on the opposite side of the table from Rita. *It was Suarez.* He whispered something in the dealer's ear. Eva held her breath. The gentleman sitting to the right of the dealer vacated his seat, and Suarez took his place. He looked across the table at Rita, his dark eyes unreadable, but his half smile was unmistakable. He was going to challenge her.

The dealer dealt the next hand. Suarez lit a cigar and placed it in the ashtray next to him as he looked at his hand. His heavy lids rose; his eyes locked on Rita. She smiled and then turned her attention back to her cards.

The first hand went to Rita. The next to Suarez. The next two went to Rita. Suarez never batted an eye. He took a long pull from his cigar. The crowd was utterly silent.

"Winner take all," Suarez said, his accent as smooth and intoxicating as a good liqueur.

Rita arched a brow, surveyed her winnings. "I like a man who takes chances." She looked at the dealer. "Deal the cards and don't forget to treat the lady right." She pushed her stack of chips into the center of the table and then lit a cigarette.

Eva watched in fascination as Rita played her hand. She was either brilliant or damned lucky.

Suarez shifted the cigar from the left side of his mouth to the right as he studied his hand. His signature block diamond pinkie ring flashed with his every movement. He removed the cigar and put it in the ashtray. He looked across the table at Rita. She smiled.

Suarez slowly placed his cards on the table one by one. Ten of diamonds. Five of clubs. Five of hearts. Twenty.

All eyes turned to Rita. Jack of spades. Queen of spades. Ace of spades. Twenty-one.

A gasp rippled through the crowd.

Suarez's cheeks flushed, and then he began to laugh, a deep hearty laugh. "Beaten by a woman." He pushed up from his seat. "That must make you very special." He looked at her and at his losses one last time, turned, and disappeared into the crowd.

Rita breathed in slowly, the rush of adrenaline tapering off.

"Do you wish to play again?" the dealer asked.

Rita blinked until the room came back into focus. "Uh, no. I think that's it for me for the night."

The dealer signaled to one of the assistants, who collected her winning chips on a tray and escorted her to the cashier.

Eva decided to follow Suarez. She hurried around the crowd, trying to spot him. She caught a glimpse of him as he and his two bodyguards went up the escalator.

"Jake," she said into her headset. "You and Jinx need to get down here."

"I'm on my way," Jake replied, tucking his shirt into his pants. "What's up?"

"Let's just say that Rita beat the hell outta Suarez at

blackjack, and he's just left the casino. He's headed up. I'm on the escalator following him."

"Cool. Keep him in your sights. Where's Rita?"

"Collecting her winnings."

"Hmm. That might be a good thing. Listen, forget Suarez for a minute. Go find Rita. Tell her that she wants her winnings *cashed and kept in the ship safe.*"

Eva smiled in understanding. "Right. Perfect. I'm on my way."

Jinx listened to the exchange. His heart sank. This was only step one for Rita.

Eva returned to the casino and went directly to the cashier. She spoke into her headset to Rita, who once again didn't respond. She must have taken out her earpiece, Eva realized.

Eva looked around. She needed some way to get Rita's attention without causing too much of a scene, especially at the cashier booth. One of the passing waiters put down his full tray of empty glasses on one of the rolling carts. Eva picked it up and headed in Rita's direction.

She got close enough to bump into her with the tray, rattling the glasses that rested on top of it.

Rita turned, her faced painted in annoyance until she saw that it was Eva.

"I'm so sorry," Eva said. "Put it in the safe," she whispered.

Rita's eyes widened ever so slightly; then understanding kicked in. "Sure, no problem. It was probably my fault anyway."

Eva smiled and walked away. "Done," she said into her headset.

"I'm on the pool deck," Jinx said. "Suarez and company are at the pool bar."

"Good. I'm going to swing by the room," Jake said. "See if he has anyone standing watch. One of them is missing."

"I see man number three, now," Eva said. "He's heading for Rita at the cashier's booth."

The man tapped Rita on the shoulder as she finished up her paperwork. Slowly she turned around. Eva wished she could read lips. Rita smiled brightly and nodded her head. She slipped her arm through the crook in his, and they walked off.

"They're leaving together," Eva said.

"Stay with them," Jake instructed.

Rita and the bodyguard headed for the escalator.

20

Rita walked onto the pool deck and was escorted over to where Suarez sat at the bar.

"Ahh, the woman who took my money," he said, his eyes roving over Rita. "Please," he extended his hand toward the empty seat next to him. "Join me."

Rita's slow smile was full of promise. "That's very gracious from a man who just lost almost ten thousand dollars," she said, sitting down and crossing her long legs at the knee. She put her purse on the smooth mahogany bar and turned her full attention on Suarez.

Suarez's gaze dropped to Rita's legs, caressed them for a moment before returning to rest on her face. "What are you drinking?"

"Martini . . . two olives." She licked her lips and felt her clit snap to attention when Suarez's smoky eyes darkened with intent.

Suarez's sidekick signaled for the bartender and ordered Rita's drink.

"You will have dinner with me tonight," Suarez said.

Rita cocked her right brow. "That's very presumptuous of you . . . Mr. 'I don't even know your name,'" she said like a song lyric. She popped open her purse and took out her pack of cigarettes. One was lit before she could blink. She smiled her thanks to the handy sidekick. Casually she glanced around, taking note of the location of Suarez's other two bodyguards. One was at the entrance, holding his position like the cruise ship bouncer; the second one was in the center of the dining tables on the deck, giving him full view of the comings and goings and everything in between. The third musketeer was glued to Suarez's left elbow. She saw Jinx cross the deck, pushing a cart filled with fluffy white towels. She blew a puff of smoke into the air.

"Xavier," he said, the word rolling off his tongue as smooth as the finest Godiva chocolate: thick, rich, and totally decadent.

"I knew a man named Xavier once." She paused, took a sip of her martini. "But he didn't look anything like you," she said, the words floating on a heavy breath.

Xavier chuckled. "I will take that as a compliment." He stood. "Come, our table is ready." He took her hand while she stood. His assistant picked up her drink and followed them. "You look quite lovely. Did I mention that?"

Rita turned to him as they approached the exit of the pool deck. "You just did." She smiled, hesitated for a moment. "Oh, I thought we were staying up here."

"No. I have a private table reserved in the restaurant." He waved his hand in a dismissive fashion. "This is much too busy. I want to hear every word you have to say. And maybe you will even tell me your name . . . before the night is over."

"They're leaving the pool deck," Jinx murmured into his headset as he circled the pool, picking up the wet discarded towels and dumping them into the laundry bag hanging from beneath his cart.

"I'm going to check out the room," Jake said. "Jinx, keep an eye on Rita. Eva meet me up on eleven."

Eva walked a U-turn in the direction of the elevator. She wanted to tell Jake to let Jinx go with him to Suarez's room. She wanted to keep an eye on Rita herself. She sighed, pushing her lips together in concentration as she waited for the elevator. That bad feeling she had at the very beginning of this gig still had not gone away.

The elevator doors swooshed open, and she sucked in a lungful of shock.

"Eva?" The woman in front of her frowned with concentration, trying to peer beyond the black wig and employee uniform. "Eva Kelly?"

Eva's pulse beat so loud in her ears, she felt as if she were underwater. She ignored the woman and stepped onto the elevator as the woman stepped off, never taking her eyes off Eva even as she was pushed along by the exiting passengers.

Eva held her breath, kept her gaze fixed on the elevator floor, and willed the doors to close. By the time she reached the eleventh level, she'd stopped shaking enough to be able to walk down the corridor without her legs giving out from under her.

Jake was in the corridor with a dust cloth in his hand, polishing the brass railing that ran the length of the walkway.

Eva tugged in a breath and approached. She walked past him and stopped opposite Suarez's room. She knocked on the door under the pretext of being from the hospitality staff.

There was no answer.

Jake pulled a decoder out of his pocket. It was no bigger than a BlackBerry device.

"Watch the hall," he said.

Eva took the dust cloth from him and picked up where he'd left off.

Jake stepped up to the door lock, inserted a blank plastic card in the lock, and then keyed in a series of numbers into the decoder.

The lock clicked. He smiled, turned the handle, but the door wouldn't open.

"What's wrong?" Eva whispered.

"Not opening." He repeated the steps, making sure the card and the magnetic strip were lined up properly. The lock clicked. He tried the handle.

"Shit," he spat. He shook the handle again. No luck.

"Come on. We better go before someone sees us," Eva urged.

Jake stuck the device and card back in his pocket and followed Eva down the hallway to the elevator. "If I can't get this to work, we're going to have to get the key from Suarez."

"That's not the only problem we have," Eva said, pushing the DOWN button for the elevator.

Jake groaned. "I'm not sure I want to know."

She folded her arms to keep from punching him. "Well, that's just too damned bad."

The elevator door opened, and they stepped inside. The only thing keeping her from slapping him in the back of the head was the old wrinkled couple that was already on board.

They walked in silence to their cabin.

"All right, so what is it?" Jake asked, shutting the door and tossing the gadget on the bed in almost the same movement.

Eva spun toward him. "Traci is on the ship."

Jake figured it must be some woman thing. 'Cause he just didn't get it. "Who is Traci?" he breathed in frustration.

Eva planted her fists at her waist. "Traci Jennings!" *You idiot* is what it sounded like to Jake. His brow creased in concentration. For the life of him, he couldn't recall a Traci anybody.

Eva's chest rose and fell hard. She pulled the wig from her head and tossed it on the bed, eyeing him with fury. Jake knew she was about to lose it, and his *Jeopardy!* minute was running out.

He threw his hands up in the air. "I give up. You gotta tell me who Traci Jennings is."

"Traci Jennings is Sebastian's ex-girlfriend. And if you recall, Sebastian is my *boss*." Her eyes widened to emphasize her point.

Jake's face went through a short series of contortions as the information sank in. "Shit," he finally sputtered.

"Yeah, my sentiments exactly."

They sat down on the bed like synchronized swimmers, in perfect unison.

"Maybe we should just jump overboard, cut our losses, and hope to be rescued by a friendly pirate," Eva said without a stitch of humor in her voice.

Jake leaned forward, rested his chin in his palm. "Did she recognize you?"

Eva nodded. "She called me by name."

Jake turned to her. "What did you do?"

"Ignored her. She was getting off the elevator while I was getting on to come and meet you."

"Not something we bargained on," he said absently.

"I have two choices. I can either stay cooped up in this room until we dock or I can do what I came here to do. We're already shorthanded, so item number one is not an option."

"We can't afford to have this Traci chick cause us any problem."

"I'll take care of her if I run into her again."

"Do you think she'll say something to Sebastian?"

Eva sighed heavily. "No. Yes. I don't know. If she does, I'll just have to deal with it when the time comes." She ran her hand across her head and pulled off the stocking cap that held her hair in place. She tossed it down on the bed with the wig.

She jerked her chin toward the decoder. "What happened?"

Jake shook his head. "Something I missed in the program."

"Is that going to be the same problem we have getting into the safe?" She didn't mean for it to sound facetious. Well, maybe she did.

Jake cut his eyes in her direction. "That's not the plan." He stood up, went to the minibar, and fixed a quick drink. "Want one?" he asked with his back to her.

"No. Thanks." She braced her arms on her thighs and entwined her fingers. "We've gone through too much to prepare for this to get screwed by some fluke coincidence," she said.

Jake turned, leaned against the bar, and took a sip from his drink. "What are you thinking?"

"I'm thinking . . ." Her voice suddenly broke. She looked up at Jake, and her eyes filled. She sniffed. "I'm thinking that I want this to be over, Jake. I want to go home. I don't want to do this anymore." She jumped up. "The hell with the sting. When we dock in Mexico, let's just keep going." Her eyes ran over his face.

He'd never seen her like this before. Eva may be tempermental at times, but it was always only directed at him. No job had ever rattled her. Eva was always cool—indifferent almost—when she executed a plan. More than just a few glitches in the plan were eating at her.

He crossed the room and sat down next to her. She was holding her body so tight, he was afraid if he held her she would snap.

"Talk to me," he said gently.

"It's . . . just all wrong," she sputtered, sniffing and wiping her eyes. "Everything. This whole thing has been a problem from day one, and it's only getting worse."

"We've been in fixes before. You never even blinked. Why now?"

She pulled in a shuddering breath. She turned and looked into her husband's eyes. "Don't you ever think about the people we fuck over?"

"No. Not really."

Her mouth jerked slightly. The almost-smile faded. "Most of the time I don't either. I always figured I'd been fucked over since long before I knew that's what was happening to me, so why not return the favor tenfold. Ya know."

Jake nodded but kept silent, letting her get it out, whatever it was.

She shrugged slightly. "Now it seems like it's all coming back to kick us in the ass. Reaping what you sow. Know what I mean?"

"You know I don't go in for all that karma and religious bullshit," he said half-grudgingly. "But things have been more than a little shady with this job."

"And Jake . . . I don't want to . . . have this baby in jail or spend the rest of our lives running with our child." She swallowed. There. She'd said it, said it before she changed her mind. Said it, said it, made it real. It wasn't just the plus sign in a slender white tube that she'd seen and didn't want to believe earlier that morning. It was real because she'd said it. Said it. She breathed in and out, slow and deep. Waited.

Of course she was kidding. *Eva* plus *Jake* didn't equal *baby*. They'd talked about it. She knew how he felt. He couldn't be any baby's daddy. It wasn't in the genes. Hadn't his daddy proved that? According to his mother, things were great between her and him until Jake and John were born with barely a year between deliveries.

He could still hear his mother crying when the beatings started. How he used to hold Jinx tight against his chest, trying to cover his ears, shielding him from the screaming and cussing. How many times did he stand in front of his father and listen to him tell him what a little piece of shit he was that ruined his life. "Kids ruin lives. Don't forget that, boy." A thick, callused finger wagged in his face. "They drain you. Take everything from you. Just like you and your whining-ass brother."

If Jake was really good and didn't cry, maybe he'd only get punched in the stomach instead of tossed against the wall. "Make you tough," his father would say when he beat him. And when his mother would tiptoe into their room late at night after headboard-banging sex with his father, she'd sit on the side of his bed, stroke his hair, and tell him how much he looked like his daddy. "Must be some strong genes that man has," she'd say, almost wistful.

It's in the genes. And he had no intention of passing those genes along.

His jaw locked. If he said anything now . . . He put his glass down on the table and walked out of the cabin.

Eva covered her face with her hands, letting tears slip between her fingers. When she'd finished crying, she got up, went to the bathroom, and washed her face. She reapplied her makeup, put the stocking cap and wig back on, adjusted her headset, and walked out.

She wouldn't be the first single mom, and she damn sure wouldn't be the last. She walked with purpose down the hall, passing one of the cleaning staff in the corridor. She gently bumped the worker, mumbled her apologies, and kept going. She slid the master key card in her pocket. *Fuck you, Jake Kelly. I'll take my cut, and cut your ass loose.*

She pressed the elevator, got on, then disembarked on the eleventh floor.

Eva checked the hallway. Cruise guests came and went, paying her no attention. After all, she was only a crew member—invisible.

She knocked once on Suarez's door. No answer. She knocked again. Adrenaline and anger rushed through her veins, pounding in her head.

She drew in a breath, stuck the key in the slot. The green light flashed. She turned the lock and stepped inside Xavier Suarez's suite.

21

"Were you visiting Brazil for business or pleasure?" Xavier asked Rita as he sipped his glass of wine.

"I try to include pleasure in everything that I do." She cut into her grilled salmon. "And you?"

He chuckled. "I was born in Venezuela. Brazil is my home now. I wish I could have shown you my beautiful country."

"Perhaps another time." Her statement held the note of a question.

"I'd like that very much. Is Miami home?"

"No. I live in New York."

"I can't imagine that a beautiful woman such as you is traveling alone."

"New York women are very independent." She put a piece of salmon in her mouth, chewed slowly as she looked at him.

"I admire independence in a woman. It gives them fire."

"Is that right?"

"Perhaps you would honor me by proving my point."

It was Rita's turn to laugh. "That can be taken several ways, Xavier." She loved saying his name.

He raised his glass in a toast. "To proving my point."

She touched her glass to his.

Jinx stood along the perimeter of the restaurant. He had Rita and Suarez in sight—and didn't like the view one bit. Rita looked too happy, too engaged, too sensual. He cringed each time she leaned forward, giving Suarez a whiff of her deep cleavage, or when she tossed her head back and laughed, revealing the long sleek slope of her neck.

This was supposed to be a job, and he knew she was good at what she did, but he'd never seen her in action. And from his standpoint, she didn't appear as if she was working at all. It looked like she was on a date in the company of a man whose presence she enjoyed.

Suarez reached across the table and lifted a curl away from Rita's face. Jinx's temples pounded. He snatched up a circular tray from the rack and made his way to their table.

"Can I take anything away?" he said upon reaching the table.

Suarez looked up at him. Anger darkened his eyes. "When we are ready, I will let you know." His sidekick appeared out of nowhere, coming between Suarez and Jinx like a drawn curtain. Suarez threw up his hand to stop his forward motion.

Rita held her breath. It was like watching a movie when the good and bad guys square off and draw their guns.

"Of course." He gave a short incline of his head before stealing a look at Rita, who returned his gaze as if he were a perfect stranger. He turned and walked away, his insides on fire.

"At least the service is good," Rita said, hoping that Xavier didn't notice her hand shaking when she put down her fork. What the hell was Jinx thinking?

"I do not like being disturbed when I'm entertaining," he said, his clipped tone sending a thrill through her.

Her mouth went dry. She forced herself to smile. "I admire a man who knows what he wants," she said, hoping to soften the suddenly tense atmosphere. She wiped the corners of her mouth with the stiff white linen napkin.

The hard lines around his eyes and mouth slowly diminished. "I apologize for that," he said, slipping effortlessly back into the role of polished gentleman.

"I'm sure he was only doing his job."

His mouth flickered with the beginnings of a smile. "I'm sure." He lifted his wineglass to his mouth and sipped slowly, never taking his eyes from Rita. "I hope that you will join me for the rest of the evening. I understand there is a wonderful show in the nightclub."

"I'd like that very much."

"But I would like to know the name of the lovely woman that I am spending my time and my money on."

"Rita. Rita Davis."

Eva closed the cabin door behind her and walked into the well-appointed suite. Now this was living, she thought as she took in the view of the ocean, the lush carpeting, recessed lighting, and chic contemporary furnishings. It was a full apartment, from what she could see.

She stood in the center of the room with her hands on her hips. She'd start with the bedroom.

Eva moved slowly around the room. Her first stop was the built-in closet. The hanger rod was thick with clothes. On the floor were two suitcases. She pulled them out, sat down, and opened the first one, since it didn't have a lock like the second one.

It was filled with folders and an array of passports, all with Xavier's face with different names.

Interesting. She put the passports back and then started sifting through the folders. All the documents and letters were in Spanish and Portuguese, but they looked important. Many of them carried government or notarized seals—that much she could figure out. She wished she'd paid more attention in Spanish class. She returned the documents to the folders and put them back in the suitcase. She pulled the second one to her just as she heard a noise at the front door.

"Shit." She zipped the suitcase closed and shoved them both back into the closet. She eased the closet door shut. The front door opened. Frantic, she looked around.

There was no way out.

Jake had been on every level since he'd left the cabin—and Eva. He didn't see her anywhere, and she wasn't picking up her headset.

He'd probably have to sleep on the floor. He deserved it. The least he could have done was respond to her. But he'd been so stunned by the information, he knew that whatever he said at that moment would be the wrong thing.

How could he, in good conscience, bring a child into the world? He couldn't. Wouldn't risk it. Not even for Eva.

His stomach rocked back and forth. He felt ill, weak, and defenseless. All the things he never wanted to be for his wife.

Jake wandered aimlessly through the ship, taking in the

happy faces, the families, the couples old and young. He slung his hands in his pockets.

The guilt of Earl's death, fear and trauma of it that he carried around inside all these years was enough of a confession, enough of a breach of his maleness. What little he had learned about being a man came from the street, from watching the OGs, the original gangsters, do their thing. He watched how they lived—on the edge, full out. There was no weakness, no room for compromise. And you never loved anyone more than yourself or the game. If you did, that's when it got dangerous. When you let your guard down, you opened the door for the enemy. And the enemy seeing your weakness could hurt you—through them.

He'd broken the cardinal rule by loving Eva so hard. She was his Achilles' heel, his weakness. One was enough. A child was out of the question. And then there was always the dark fact that any child of his would carry his father's genes—and that he especially couldn't abide—not even for Eva. She'd have to go see someone as soon as they got back. Make it go away. Then they could pick up where they'd left off and put this whole baby thing behind them.

Jake and Jinx made a pact years ago that they'd never bring any children in the world—that the cursed Kelly line would end with them. Until now, neither of them had broken that promise.

"They left the restaurant," Jinx whispered in Jake's ear, snapping him out of his troubling thoughts.

"Yeah, Jinx," he muttered, coming to. "Where are they going?"

"Don't know."

Don't know. "Aren't you following them?"

Silence.

"Jinx." Jake hissed the word into his headset. He looked

around, found a quiet corner next to a fake palm tree that was at least three stories tall. "What's going on?"

"Maybe you need to ask Rita."

Jake's thick brows drew together. "Look, what are you talking about? What happened?"

"I'm going to get a drink."

"Jinx. Where are you?"

"On the pool deck," he said, his tone devoid of any emotion.

"I'm on my way. Stay put."

Jake dodged guests, went up escalators and around waiters and waitresses. He spotted Jinx at the entrance to the pool deck.

"What's going on, man?" he asked his brother, coming up alongside him.

Jinx lowered his eyes. "You shoulda seen her, man."

"Rita?"

His face twisted into a nasty grimace. "Who the hell you *think* I'm talking about?"

"Yo, Jinx, man, you need to chill. This is me."

Jinx jerked his shoulder as if snatching it out of some invisible grasp. "Yeah, I know it's you. It's always been about you. We wouldn't be here if it wasn't for you, and Rita wouldn't be all in Suarez's pants if it wasn't for you!" He spat out the last word as it if were a curse.

Jake flinched. "You want to tell me what's really going on? Rita is doing her job. This is a job, remember?"

Jinx turned somber eyes on his brother. He appeared to deflate. His shoulders slumped; the fire in his eyes dimmed. "I didn't ever think it would be like this." He tried to smile and failed. "We aren't supposed to be the soft guys that fall for the girl. We're the tough guys that the girls fall for." His laugh fell flat.

Jake held his tongue and let Jinx talk.

"I'm not even sure when it hit me that I was in love with her. It was all of a sudden, ya know. Like a freak flash flood or something." He shook his head, short and quick. "And I feel like I'm drowning."

Jake leaned his back against the wall, stared out toward the guests swimming in the pool. "Eva's pregnant."

Jinx turned to his brother, the promise they'd made hovering in his eyes. "Well, my brotha, looks like we're both in a bit of a fix."

"You know that drink you were talking about sounds really good right about now."

"Don't feel like dealing with the crowd and the noise," Jinx said.

"Let's go back to my cabin. We need to get out of these outfits anyway before someone notices that we aren't actually working."

When they returned to the cabin, Jake fixed them both a drink. Just as they turned up their glasses, the cell phone rang. Jake cut his eyes at Jinx and then flipped open the phone.

"Yeah," Jake said. He listened for a few minutes then hung up. He glanced at Jinx.

"What now?"

"She's changed the drop spot again. Back to the original location—Miami."

Jinx tossed the contents of his glass down his throat. "Bitch," he blurted.

"Touché, Ms. Ingram."

The front door to Suarez's room shut. Eva heard movement coming from the living room area. The window was too small and would take too much work and noise to get out of it. Not to mention the looks she'd get jumping out of a window and onto the deck.

She opted for the closet, tucked herself far into the back, and squatted down on the floor—and none too soon. The bedroom door opened, and Xavier and Rita came in.

22

Jake sat in the side chair, and Jinx took a seat on the edge of the bed. Both had a drink in their hands.

"You're really twisted about Rita, huh?" Jake asked after a long silence between the two brothers.

Jinx looked up. "Yeah."

"Does she know how you feel?"

"Not really. I mean I know she understands that I care about her. . . ."

"How does she feel about you?"

"Hmph, with Rita, who knows? She doesn't ever say how she feels. For all I know, I'm just another job."

"They're both cut from the same cloth, like me and you. They had it rough coming up."

Jinx took a long swallow from his drink. "Yeah, but we weren't supposed to get caught up in the love thing, ya know?"

Jake nodded slowly.

"That's why you totally blew me away when you actually married Eva." He looked into his brother's eyes. "I figured it was just for the sex. But sometimes I look at you when you're watching her, and it's in your eyes, man. You love her."

Jake looked away. It was true: he did love his wife, and it made him crazy. It was his weak spot, and he wasn't supposed to have any. And now this baby thing . . .

"So what are you going to do, man?" Jinx asked, as if reading his mind.

"Eva's been hinting for a while that she wanted to get out of the game. I figured it would pass, ya know. I mean, this is what we do. It's what brought us together." He glanced off into the distance, shook his head in confusion. "I just don't know. I don't think I can handle it." He looked into his brother's eyes. "It scares me, John. What if I turn out like our father?"

Jinx grimaced, the horrors of their youth flashing before his eyes. He remembered that Jake was always there to protect him, promised that he'd take care of him no matter what. And he'd never broken that promise in all these years.

"Look, we may have his genes, but we're nothing like him. You're nothing like him. You've proved that over the years. Do you think that if you were the man our father was, you would have cared about me all this time, gotten me out of scrapes, made sure that I finished school? You didn't turn your back on me when I went to jail. You stood by me." He paused. "And if you were anything like him, you wouldn't give a damn about Eva being pregnant. It wouldn't touch you. It wouldn't worry you. The only emotions our father had were bitterness and anger. And that's not you, man. He didn't know how to love anything. You do. Don't blow it."

A half smile widened Jake's mouth. "Never thought I'd get a life lesson from my baby brother."

Jinx chuckled. "I'm all grown up now. Maybe it's time we let go of the past. Forget some of those 'survival' promises we made, ya know. You got a great woman, and I have one that I want to make mine. We can either step up to the plate and go for it or let them go and keep living the way we've been living. For me, I'm ready to start living a new life."

Jake listened to his brother's words. Maybe he was right. Maybe it was time to let go of the past and move on. This was just supposed to be another job, but every step of the way had offered a new revelation. He'd been forced to confront things about himself and his relationship with his wife that he'd otherwise been able to avoid. He sighed heavily, stood, and went to refill his glass.

"I told Eva about that day at the beach," he said, his tone quiet and pensive.

Jinx was silent for a moment. "What did she say?"

"Said it wasn't my fault and that I had to let it go, couldn't hold on to the guilt." He turned to Jinx. "She didn't blame me."

"Something you'd been doing to yourself for years."

"Yeah. It messed with me. It really did. Made me over-protective, overly cautious, guarded. And at the same time, I lived on the edge with everything that I did, almost as if I wanted to live dangerously—with the secret thought that I'd get caught and pay for what I'd done."

"You know what? You don't need a brother and a drink—you need a psychiatrist," Jinx joked. He got up, crossed the room, and slapped Jake on the back. "You got issues."

Jake laughed. "You're probably right."

"But—" He held up a finger. "—you got a good woman who's willing to put up with all your bullshit and your phobias."

Jake grinned. "Yeah, I do, don't I?"

Jinx's expression grew serious. "Don't blow it. Besides, I kinda like the thought of being Uncle Jinx. Has a nice ring to it, don't ya think?"

Suddenly the whole notion of becoming a father filled him with a sense of awe. The weight and responsibility of bringing into the world and shaping the life of another human being was the biggest challenge he would ever face. He knew all about cracking computer codes, breaking and entering the most secure locations. But being a father, a daddy, was not for him. That was a job he couldn't afford to fuck up.

"Me and Eva are gonna have to deal with it when we get this job out of the way and we're in the clear. No point in planning for a future that I'm uncertain about."

Jinx slowly put down his drink on the nightstand. "What do you mean . . . uncertain?"

Jake lowered his head. "We have a little problem." He looked up and told Jinx about the codes for the safe. "But now that Rita's substantial winnings are locked up in the ship's safe, we have a good opportunity to get in there. We're going to have to plan to make the switch when she goes in there."

Jinx nodded in agreement. "Yeah, we let Rita go in first to check on her winnings and to check out the system."

"Right. And when it's time, Rita will make the switch."

"If Suarez's stuff is even in there. What if it's in his suite?"

"It'll be a helluva lot easier getting into his suite than the ship's safe." At least he hoped so, considering his earlier fiasco with the cabin lock.

Jinx finished off his drink. "Speaking of the women in our lives . . ."

"Yeah, let's go find our women."

Eva held her breath and her body in a tight ball. She didn't dare move an inch and silently prayed that Suarez wasn't coming into the room to change clothes.

"You certainly travel in high style," she heard Rita say.

"Only the best," Suarez responded.

The closet door suddenly opened. Eva almost gasped.

Suarez pulled a silk robe from the hanger and closed the door.

Eva closed her eyes and shook in relief. What in the world was she thinking coming here without letting anyone know where she was?

"I'm going to change." He smiled full of innuendo. "Make yourself comfortable in the meantime."

Eva heard the bathroom door open and then close. Should she risk revealing herself to Rita?

She eased the closet door open. Rita was on the far side of the room, going through the items on the top of the dresser.

"Psst, Rita . . ."

Rita jumped, dropping the wallet on top of the dresser. She spun around. Her eyes widened in alarm then darted toward the bathroom door.

She hurried across the room, keeping a lookout on the bathroom.

"What are you doing here?" she whispered.

Eva peeked out from behind the row of suits. "Seeing what I could find. Where are his bodyguards?"

"One is out in front of the door. Don't know about the other two."

"You gotta get him out of here and keep him busy. So whatever you had on your mind, forget it, Rita. Understood?" she said in no uncertain terms.

Rita vigorously nodded her head. "Just be quiet and stay out of sight." Rita straightened and quietly shut the door. She quickly crossed the room and sat in the chair by the bed, composing herself just as Suarez emerged from the bathroom.

"I'm sure I can find something that you would be more comfortable in."

She licked her lips. "Oh, I had my heart set on going to the show. I thought that was the plan."

Suarez walked up to her, lifted her chin with the tip of his finger. "Plans can always be changed."

Her insides melted; her resolve faltered. She wanted him, but she didn't want to arouse his suspicions. Too much was at stake. But then she pictured her cousin crouched in the closet. Could Eva sit there and be quiet while she and Suarez got wet and wild on his king-size bed?

She took a step back. "Of course plans can be changed. I enjoy spontaneity in a man. But I did have my heart set on the show, especially after you recommended it." She drew in a breath and stepped closer. "And you don't seem to be the kind of man that would disappoint a lady." She drew a long nail tantalizingly down the center of his exposed chest.

Suarez's dark eyes grew even darker. His cheeks flushed beneath his even bronze complexion. "As you wish." He walked away, back into the bathroom to change.

Rita sighed in relief. She walked past the closet and out into the front room, taking a seat on the couch. She didn't want Suarez to come out of the bathroom, find her sitting on his bed, and get any ideas that she'd changed her mind.

Moments later Suarez joined her. He straightened his tie. Looking down at her, he said, "Never let anyone tell you that I didn't make a lady happy."

Damn that Eva! "No one would dare say that." She took his hand and stood.

Xavier placed a light kiss on her cheek. "I also admire a woman who has respect for herself. It forces me to respect her as well." He chuckled. "You have forced me to respect you, beautiful Rita." He brought her hand to his lips and kissed the top of it. "Respect goes a long way. Always remember that," he added, looking into her eyes. "Come. Let us go and be entertained."

Once Eva was certain that they were gone and no one else was lurking about, she crept out of the closet. She tried to stand, but her legs gave out from being crouched for so long, and she wobbled to the floor. Wincing, she stretched her legs out in front of her and massaged her thighs and calves and wiggled her toes until blood started flowing again. She would have been a permanent pretzel if the two of them had hit the sheets and she'd been stuck in the closet the whole time.

At least she didn't lose her cool, she thought, slowly standing to test out her legs. The closet experience with Jake taught her well how to remain calm under pressure and not get claustrophobic and flip out.

Jake. She sighed, arched her back, then continued snooping around. She expected all sorts of reactions when she told him about being pregnant: shock, surprise, elation, maybe even anger, but not nothing. Not a word, not an outward expression of any emotion. All that nothing made her feel like she was dying inside.

She knew Jake had issues about starting a family. She opened the drawer next to the bed and gently lifted the papers inside so as not to disturb anything. But Jake had never really discussed his feelings with her. She closed the drawer then stood in the center of the room and did a slow 360, taking in the room inch by inch. She also knew he and Jinx grew up pretty much on their own much like she and Rita. All he'd ever said about his home life was that it was bad. It was a touchy subject for both of them, and so it was easy to push the past to the side and act like it didn't happen.

Eva crossed the room and went back to the closet, pulling out the locked suitcase. *People don't lock things if the stuff inside isn't important.* She could hear Jake's voice as plain as day. She fought back a smile as she studied the lock. It wasn't the lock that typically came with the suitcase. This one was specially made and from what she could see, brand-spanking-new. There were three locks on it: one on either end and one in the center. The one in the center was a combination lock. The suitcase was pretty heavy, but was it heavy enough to contain the money and the diamonds?

No way of knowing unless they could get inside it. If anyone could, it would be Jake.

She snatched a piece of paper from the complimentary notepad on the nightstand by the bed and returned to the suitcase. Her years of sketching came in handy now. She quickly drew a duplicate of the suitcase, careful to include all the minute details, particularly the combination and the assembly around the locks.

Satisfied with her handiwork, she returned the suitcase

to the closet, took one last look around to be sure she didn't leave any signs of her entry. She went to the front door, listened for any sounds, and inched the door open, then remembered that she was dressed as one of the crew. She was in uniform.

Eva opened the door fully and boldly stepped out into the corridor. She pulled the door shut behind her as two couples walked in opposite directions down the hallway, neither of them paying her any attention.

She headed back to her room. Just as she reached the cabin door, Jake and Jinx were coming out.

"Jake—"

"Eva, I'm—"

"Why don't I let you two chat." Jinx looked from one to the other before walking off.

They faced each other.

Less than an hour ago, she was ready to do it on her own. Walk away from the job and the man. But now, standing in front of him, she knew that all she'd ever wanted was Jake Kelly. But something was different.

Jake's always-ready grin, his devil-may-care charm were missing. In their place was an aura of tentativeness, a vulnerability that she rarely if ever saw. And that's when it hit her. He was afraid, not of failing at this job but at failing her. She reached out her hand and took his.

The beginning of a smile warmed his eyes. He angled his head toward the door of the cabin, and they went inside.

23

A Latin jazz band opened the show and enthusiastic party-goers took to the small dance floor doing salsa and mambo, dancing in the aisles when the floor became too crowded as they gyrated to the driving beats and sensual rhythms. Waiters couldn't keep up with the requests for drinks and refills even as they dodged around. Sequins flashed and heels clicked to the beat.

Xavier and Rita had front-row seats. Xavier saw to her every want. Drinks and food flowed throughout the evening. Xavier was the perfect gentleman and an excellent dancer. Never once did he give her the impression that he was the vicious crime lord she'd heard about.

Xavier's hand was at the small of her back as they left the lounge.

"I hope that you enjoyed yourself," Xavier said.

"I had a wonderful time. Thank you."

"Perhaps a nightcap . . . in my suite?"

She turned to him, keeping her smile in place. She reached out and ran a manicured nail across his jaw. "Another night. Maybe tomorrow? Besides, we have this entire cruise to get to know each other," she said in a husky whisper.

The right corner of his mouth flickered. He raised his hand, and his bodyguard appeared.

"See to it that the lovely Rita gets to her cabin safely."

"I'm a big girl. I'll be fine on my own. Independent, remember?"

He brought Rita's hand to his lips. "Until tomorrow, then." He turned and walked away, his other two bodyguards flanking him on either side.

Rita released a breath and walked in the opposite direction to her cabin.

When she opened the door, Jinx was sitting on the bed, like a father waiting up for his teenaged daughter to come home from a date.

She closed the door and tossed her purse on top of the dresser.

"You didn't have to wait up," she said, taking off one shoe and then the other. She put them in the closet.

"I wanted to hear about your evening."

She faced him. "Do you, really?"

"Yeah, I do."

"How about we start with you showing up at the table like some jealous boyfriend. Do you know you could have blown the whole thing?" She turned her back to him. "Unzip me, please," she asked, her tone softer.

Jinx got up and unzipped her gown in a series of slow pulls, kissing her spine with each inch that was exposed.

Rita groaned. It would be so easy to simply screw his brains out and sidestep what she was sure was coming.

He eased the spaghetti straps off one at a time, caressed her shoulders. He kissed the back of her neck and relished her soft moan.

"Maybe I was jealous," he said softly, and then unfastened the gold clip holding her hair in place. Her hair fell in soft waves across her shoulders. "Would that surprise you?"

"Yesss, it would." She arched her neck while his hands glided over her hips.

"Why? Don't you know how I feel about you, Rita?"

She turned around into his arms, looked into his questioning eyes. "No. I don't know how you feel about me."

The statement was so innocent, it took Jinx by surprise. "How could you not know, baby? Tell me how you couldn't know."

Rita lowered her head. "Because no one ever cared about me, Jinx." She looked straight into his eyes. "Nobody but Eva. Men wanted me for what they thought they could get between my legs, and I guess I thought that was some kind of love, ya know." She moved away from him to the other side of the room.

"I'm not other guys, Rita. I thought you knew that by now."

Pain showed in her eyes when she looked at him. "I don't know how to be any other way than the way I am—who I am." She turned away.

"I wouldn't want you any other way. I know about your past, and I don't care."

She vigorously shook her head. "No, you don't." Her arms instinctively wrapped around her body. Why couldn't they just fuck and forget all this introspection?

Jinx came up behind her. Cautiously he put a hand on

her shoulder. "Then tell me, Rita. I want to know what you think I don't already. And whatever it is, I guarantee you: it won't matter. What will matter is that you've let it go and trusted me enough to put it in my hands."

Something inside her broke—the wall, the distance, the lock on her heart. She couldn't be sure. All she knew was that she couldn't hold the floodgates closed any longer. She didn't want to.

She crossed the room and slowly sat down on the side of the bed. She folded her hands in her lap, the top of her dress held up by the rise of her breasts.

"It was never easy . . . ," she began.

"I was worried," Jake said, keeping his voice even as his wife paced the room.

"No need. I can take care of myself." She looked at him. "Most of the time," she added, her voice cracking. She swallowed. "But I don't want to. I want us to take care of each other, Jake."

He came up to her, ready to grab her and make all the worry in her face go away. But he hesitated. Sex had always been the quick fix, the easy remedy, the turn-on that turned everything else in their life off—at least temporarily. And as much as he wanted her, he didn't want the real issue between them to get murky, obscured by lust.

"So do I," he admitted. He slid his hands into the pockets of his pants.

Eva expected him to reach for her, to hold her and tell her how sorry he was. Instead he acted as if he didn't want to be near her. Her stomach knotted with dread. She drew in a breath then turned her back to him.

"I got inside Suarez's cabin." There, they were back on solid, familiar ground.

Jake frowned, unsure he'd heard her correctly. "You did what?"

"I got in his cabin." She pulled the piece of paper with the sketch out of her pocket and tossed it on the end table. "That's the suitcase that I found stashed in the closet."

Jake barely glanced at it from his side of the room. He was still working on putting together in his head what she'd told him. All this time he was worried that she was off somewhere brooding about what went down between them, and instead she was breaking and entering into Suarez's cabin—something he'd been unable to do. He wasn't sure what pissed him off more.

"You . . . you got into his cabin and got a sketch of the briefcase?"

She spun toward him, her face pinched as if her feet suddenly hurt. "What part of what I said didn't you understand?"

"The whole thing." He folded his arms across his chest. "How?"

"How what?" She snapped her neck to the side.

"How did you get in?"

"I lifted a master key card from one of the housekeeping staff like I was supposed to do from the jump." She did a mime routine of her handiwork. Her smirk was triumphant. "It's what I do."

He snorted more in amazement than annoyance. "So much for technology, huh?"

"Sometimes we have to go back to bare basics."

They looked at each other.

"I'm sorry, baby," Jake murmured. He moved toward her.

Eva withdrew from him. "What are you sorry about? Sorry about how you feel?" Slowly she shook her head. *Hold me,* she cried silently. *Hold me and tell me it's going to be all right.*

"No. That's not what I mean. I can't help how I feel, but I can help how my feelings hurt you. I don't want to hurt you. You know that."

Her gaze snapped up to meet his. "I don't know anything. I tell you that I'm pregnant. I didn't even get an 'Are you sure it's mine?' " she taunted, sarcasm turning her voice harsh and raspy. She sniffed. "So I'm not really sure what you're sorry about, Jake. And you know what? It doesn't matter." Her shoulders slumped. "You need to go over that sketch. Maybe you can figure something out. I'm going to take a shower and go to bed." She started for the bathroom. "And I'd appreciate it if you slept on the couch." She opened the bathroom door and shut it firmly behind her, turning the lock on the knob.

She pressed her forehead against the door and set free the tears that she'd been holding all night.

Rita and Jinx talked long into the night, sharing pieces of their past that they'd never told anyone other than Jake and Eva.

Rita felt suddenly lighter, as if her spirit had been set free. Jinx didn't cringe or turn away when she told him about the men, the hotels, the jobs, the money. He didn't loosen his hold of her when she told him about the sordid things she'd done and what she'd allowed to be done to her—hoping that *this* man would be the one to stay. All the time that she talked and cried and talked, he listened, murmuring softly to her, holding her tight, telling her that it was okay.

She in turn listened to him tell of his childhood, the loneliness, the fear, the having to grow up before his time, of never feeling worthwhile because there was never anyone to tell him otherwise.

"Let's make a pact," Jinx said.

"What?" Rita whispered into the night.

"Let's start our life today. Fuck what happened yesterday, last week, last year. We put all that behind us and start working on a new day."

She turned around in his arms to face him. "It's not going to be easy."

"Not much is."

"The only thing I can promise is that I'll try."

He brushed her lip with the tip of his finger. "That's all I ask." He hesitated. "I'm in love with you. Have been for a while."

She didn't respond.

"And maybe one day if you let it happen, you'll feel the same way about me."

How could she tell him that she already loved him and that she'd been running from it for years? Running and running, afraid that if she slowed down, his love would catch her. And then what would she do? She'd have to love him back . . . or leave him.

24

Jake awoke the following morning stiff and annoyed. He'd nearly fallen off the couch three times during the night, and each time his angst grew by degrees. The ship hit rocky waters during the night, and every roll and bounce increased his anxiety. Nightmares dominated what little sleep he could summon. On more than one occasion he'd crept from the couch over to the bed, hoping that Eva was awake and would tell him to join her.

In all the years they'd been together, he'd never been banished to the couch. If this was some new trend, then Eva had another thought coming. He figured he'd give her a play for one night, but that was it. She knew how hard being on this ship was for him, the old terrors that it inspired. Was this her way of getting back at him, using his confession against him? Is that what their relationship had been reduced to? Trust was a bitch. It could turn on you like a pit bull, tearing you apart until you were nothing but shreds of what you had once been.

He pulled himself up into a sitting position, hearing his joints creak in refusal to bend to his will. The shower water was running, and he had a mind to go in there and have it out with her. But good sense intervened. Eva could be pretty physical when the mood hit her. And according to statistics, the majority of in-home accidents happened in the bathroom. The fact that they were on a ship didn't ease his mind any.

The bathroom door opened. Eva stepped out, wrapped in a towel. She looked in his direction and kept walking.

"Don't I even get a good morning? How did you sleep last night?" he grumbled.

She cut her eyes in his direction. "Good morning. How did you sleep last night?" she singsonged along with her fake smile.

He stood, stretching his back as he rose. "Do you really care?"

"Frankly, my dear, I don't give a damn." She pulled open the closet and took out her clothes, tossing them on the bed.

"So this is how it's gonna be, huh?"

She whirled toward him, hands on hips. "How what's gonna be? Us? Me and you?" She craned her neck forward.

"Yeah. Us, Eva. Me and you."

She let the towel fall, waited a beat to let his eyes feast on her curves.

Heat flushed his body. He started toward her. She held up her hand, halting him in his steps.

"Take a good look, Jake, because this is the last time you'll be seeing me like this."

Slowly she bent and picked up the towel. Then she draped it back around her body. "From now on, Jake Kelly, it's strictly business between me and you." She picked up her clothes from the bed and returned to the bathroom to get dressed, slamming the door behind her.

His jaw clenched so hard, his head began to pound. Had she lost her natural mind? He was her husband, damnit! Not some stiff she picked up in a bar. Although that is how they met. But that was beside the point.

He stormed over to the bathroom and jerked on the doorknob only to find the door locked. He pounded on the door.

"Eva! Open the door. We need to talk."

She snatched the door open, and he nearly tumbled inside. "There's nothing to talk about," she said with a haughty lift of her chin. She brushed by him.

"Eva . . . please. Don't do this. There's stuff . . . that you don't understand."

Eva drew in a breath and turned slowly around. "What is it that I don't understand, Jake? Tell me."

He spat out a laugh with no humor in it. "So you can throw that back in my face too?"

"What are you talking about?"

"I'm talking about . . . what I told you about the beach and the water and my fears and guilt." He swallowed. "And last night . . ."

Her hard stance eased as she recalled how the ship pitched and rocked during the night. The thought of putting him on the couch so he could suffer wasn't part of her agenda. She wanted him to miss her and realize how he'd hurt her. She told him as much. "I wanted to teach you a lesson, but that wasn't it. I wanted you to want me, to miss me."

He sat down on the chair by the bed, but said nothing.

"I may be a bitch sometimes, but I wouldn't do that to

you." She came around to kneel down in front of him. "You hurt me, Jake. Bad."

He nodded. "You know I didn't mean to. I wouldn't do that." He reached out and stroked her hair.

She rested her hand on his lap. "But it still hurt. What are we going to do?"

It was a question he still wasn't ready to answer. "We'll work it out."

She raised her head. "What does that mean?"

He swallowed. "If this . . . baby is what you want . . . then we'll work it out."

She jumped up so fast, she nearly knocked him over. "If it's what *I* want! I didn't screw myself and make this baby. *We* did it together!"

He turned away from the truth and accusation flashing a warning in her eyes. He wanted to get the words out, to explain. But he'd broken his oath to himself once already by allowing her beyond the barricades of his past. He wouldn't do that again.

Jake straightened his shoulders and stood, forcing her to look up at him. "I told you I was sorry for hurting you. I don't have a thing to add to that. Now if you want it to be business only between us, then so be it. We get this job done, split the profits, and then . . ." He shrugged, seeming not to have a care in the world. "The rest is up to you."

Eva stayed crouched on her knees, looking up at this man whom she'd adored, loved, and admired for so long. Who the hell was he?

She pushed herself up to a standing position and walked right up to him, so close, her breasts pressed up against his chest.

"Fuck you, Jake Kelly," she said in a deadly whisper. "Fuck you straight to hell."

She grabbed her cell phone, put on her shoes, hooked up her headset, and was gone so fast, the heat of her words still hung in the air.

Jake stood in the center of the empty room. The emptiness of it as much a metaphor for his life as the reality of the environment.

"Fuck me, then," he said, his focus returning. He had a job to do. He was going to do it, get them out of this mess, and . . . And what, live a life without Eva?

He glanced toward the door. He would accept that if he had to.

Jake crossed the room to where Eva had tossed the sketch of the suitcase. He picked it up. He had to admit, it was damned good. The detailing was precise enough to be a snapshot.

He sat down and studied the sketch, then took it to the portable scanner and scanned it into the computer. Once he had the picture loaded into the computer, he enhanced the details and used a virtual simulation program to make it three-dimensional. He keyed in several equations to get an estimate of weight. According to what the computer spewed out, the suitcase weighed approximately sixty-five pounds.

He sat back, ran his hand across his chin while he stared at the screen. *Sixty-five pounds*. He quickly keyed in another set of variables.

Slowly he nodded his head as the numeric possibilities spread across the screen.

Based on the information he'd keyed in, the weight of the suitcase was consistent with the two million in cash—large bills, of course—and forty mil in diamonds. Either that or Suarez had a shitload of dirty laundry.

Still, they couldn't take the risk of simply lifting the

suitcase without knowing for sure that the stash was actually in there. The reality was, Suarez could have split up the goods: half in the suitcase and the other half in the ship safe. Jake didn't even want to entertain the thought that maybe Suarez didn't have the goods with him at all, but that one of his boys had it.

No. Suarez was too cautious. He'd never turn over that much loot to some bodyguard. He'd want to keep it close to him.

They'd just have to get into the suitcase to know for sure.

Jake peered closer at the computer screen, studying the locks, particularly the one in the middle with the combination. It would take him a few hours, but he was pretty sure he could figure out the combination. He hoped so, anyway. The image of Eva pantomiming her lifting the card key from the housekeeper and getting into the suite sat on his shoulder, mocking him. He swatted the image away.

Sure, she was an excellent pickpocket. No one could match her on that score. But he was an expert on locks and alarms. One slip did not a slouch make. He'd figure out this combination, and then they were in there. Simple. Right?

Eva went to one of the restaurants on the upper deck. She was starving. She joined the buffet line and began loading her plate. Food was a comfort, and she needed all the comforting she could stomach at the moment.

She still couldn't believe that Jake had acted so cold. She scooped a large spoonful of eggs onto her plate followed by a heaping dollop of grits. Being a single parent had never crossed her mind. Being a parent period was something that had for years been a nonissue. She inspected the bacon but then decided on sausages. She inched down the line of hungry travelers.

But lately she'd been feeling different. She wanted something more substantial than the next job. She wanted her life to mean something. Maybe there was some truth to the whole biological clock thing.

She approached the refreshment section of the buffet line. Instinctively she reached for coffee and then stopped midway. She had a baby to think about now, and so she filled her mug with orange juice instead. *A baby.* Damn. She smiled to herself, thinking of the life growing inside her. What kind of mother would she be? Better than her own was her immediate thought. Never would she treat her child the way she was treated. She'd spoil it and love it unconditionally, make him or her feel special every single day.

She took her food and found an empty table near the rear of the restaurant and began to dig in. Her stomach sighed in delight.

She should have told Jake that she'd stopped taking her birth control two months earlier. Why hadn't she? She lifted a forkful of eggs to her mouth and chewed thoughtfully. Because she knew what he would say.

Still, there was that part of her that was willing to take the risk, a part of her that hoped that Jake would be as excited as she was.

But he wasn't.

Her stomach suddenly heaved in protest. A cold sweat broke out across her forehead, and her mind felt like mush. The room moved in and out of focus. She was going to be sick.

"Eva! I knew that was you."

Eva lifted her eyes. She was definitely going to be sick.

25

Jake called Jinx on his cell phone. There always had to be a Plan B in the event that Plan A fell apart, he thought as he listened to the phone ring on the other end.

Finally Jinx picked up.

"You sound like you're just waking up, my brother," Jake said.

Jinx glanced over his shoulder. Rita was still asleep. They'd had one helluva night, and his body was still humming. He gently lifted the sheet from his body and sneaked out of the room so as not to disturb her.

"Hey, what's up?" he said, his voice still sleepy.

"I need Rita to make a visit to the safe today. We need to get in there and get a good look around. I've hooked up a microcamera that she can use undetected while she's in there."

Jinx yawned loudly and stretched. "I'll let her know. When do you want to do this?"

"Sooner rather than later. I want to have a chance to examine the pictures." He brought him up to speed regarding the sketch of the suitcase and his calculations.

Jinx chuckled. "That Eva is a master," he said.

"Hmmm. Anyway, give me a holla when she's ready."

"Hey, hold it a sec. What's going on? I hear something in your voice. Everything cool?" He scratched his head.

"Nothing. I'll work it out."

"Good, but work what out? Is it Eva? And the baby thing?"

"Something like that. Look, I really don't want to get into it right now."

"All right. Whatever you say. We'll give you a shout when Rita is ready."

"Cool." Jake disconnected the call. Slowly he put down the phone.

Generally he wouldn't have a problem kicking it with Jinx. He may not always have the best advice in the world, but he was always willing to listen—and sometimes that's all you needed.

But this was different. He couldn't even rationalize with himself why he'd acted like such an asshole. And he certainly didn't need Jinx to tell him what he already knew.

Sighing heavily, he returned his attention to the problem at hand, cracking the combination for the suitcase.

Eva hoped that the spinning in her head and stomach would slow down to a manageable level.

"Are you okay? You look perfectly ill," Traci enunciated

in that annoying New England accent—even though she was born and bred trailer trash.

Eva gulped back down the bile that had risen to her throat and washed it away with several swallows of orange juice.

Traci invited herself to sit down as if they were old friends instead of two women who secretly hated each other—at least it was a secret to everyone else.

"I was so sure that was you I saw the other day getting on the elevator." She snapped a white linen napkin open and spread it on her lap. "But then thinking about it, I decided I must be wrong. No way would our Eva be caught dead in a servant's uniform."

Our Eva. Who in the fuck was she talking about?

Traci's trilling laugh was like nails on a blackboard.

Eva cringed. "You got me there," she muttered.

Traci frowned momentarily in confusion. Then shook it off with a toss of her strawberry blond hair. "So tell me, what *are* you doing on the ship? Vacation? Business? And where is that gorgeous husband of yours?" She looked around as if expecting all the answers to her numerous questions to line up beside her.

Think girl, think. Eva rummaged through the lie she'd told Sebastian about needing the time off to look after Rita. She couldn't imagine he'd think she meant on a cruise ship. Geez, this was getting sticky. Maybe they would hit an iceberg and plunge into the ocean.

"Actually it's a mixture of business and pleasure."

Traci's thinly arched brows rose with expectation. "Oh, really?" She reached for the extra glass of water on the table and brought it to her bloodred lips. "What kind of business and pleasure?"

"The pleasure part is with my husband, and the business part is just that—business." She flashed a sneer.

"I see." Traci took another dainty sip of water. "Is Sebastian about?" She looked around again.

"No."

"Hmmm, he let you take care of business all this long way all by yourself?" Her mouth puckered in a tight line of challenge, daring Eva to cross it.

Eva put one foot across the line and then the other. She balanced her elbows on the table and leaned forward. "Let's not bullshit each other, Traci. I don't like you, and you don't like me. I think you're a gold-diggin' phony that deeply hurt a very good friend of mine, and you're still pissed 'cause I'm around and you're not. And now that we have that old business out of the way, I'd like to get back to my breakfast before it gets cold."

Traci's near alabaster complexion flushed a deep crimson, almost a perfect match to her lipstick. She jutted her chin upward, giving Eva a perfect view up her Michael Jackson nose.

She tossed down her napkin as if she'd never been insulted before and pushed back from the table. "I was only attempting to make conversation. But I see that you still lack an iota of class."

What in the name of all that's holy did Sebastian ever see in this bitch? "I missed that lesson. Now if you'll excuse me, I'm sure you have some unsuspecting fool lined up in your sights. Besides your perfume is disturbing my digestion." She proceeded to chew on a piece of sausage.

Traci spun away with a huff, muttering something about a female dog while she marched off.

Eva rolled her eyes. Her hands were shaking. She'd been so pissed off at Jake, she'd totally forgotten about looking out for Traci. *Shit, shit, shit.* She should have tried to make nice, but it wasn't in her to do so. Now she'd gone and ticked her off.

What if Traci called Sebastian just out of spite? Or just caused some yet-to-be-seen trouble just for the hell of it? *Shit, shit, shit.*

She let her fork clink onto her plate, her appetite gone. Wiping her mouth, she pushed away from the table and slowly stood, testing the readiness of her legs. At least her head had stopped spinning and her stomach was slowly settling down.

Now what? she wondered as she exited the restaurant. No messages on her cell phone, so all must be well for the time being. *Well, when in Rome, do like the Romans do.* She was going for a swim. She headed back to the cabin, determined to give Jake the cold shoulder if he was still there. All she needed to do was pick up her bathing suit and she was out.

When she walked into the cabin, Jake was busy at the computer and didn't hear her come in. For a moment she stood in the doorway watching him, wondering how things could have gotten so ugly between them.

She knew she was being stubborn and maybe even a little vindictive. It was her own guilty conscience gnawing at her, and she was taking it out on him. They'd promised each other that kids didn't factor into their lives, but she'd decided otherwise without him. She supposed he had every right to be upset. But still . . .

She shut the door. His head snapped up and then turned in her direction. Her heart stilled. *Say something, damnit.* He turned back to what he was doing.

Eva walked off to the bedroom area. She took her swimsuit from the dresser drawer, a pair of flip-flops from the closet, gave him one last look from across her shoulder, and walked back out.

Jake hung his head, feeling like a pin-pricked balloon. Why did he let her walk out? He knew why: He had no idea what to say to her.

He turned back to the computer and tried to concentrate on cracking the combination.

A light knock on the door drew his attention away from his work. He got up to answer.

"You look a little beat down," Rita said, and stepped inside.

"Thanks."

"Rough night?" Jinx asked, clapping him on the back. He'd followed Rita in.

"Something like that." He closed the door and walked inside. He went to the bed and picked up the micro digital camera and handed it to Rita.

"The pictures you take will show right up on this computer. It can take stills as well as video. Click the switch once, and it takes pictures. Hold it down for about five seconds, and the video will start to run."

Rita held the tiny gadget in her hand, turning it over. "This is some real James Bond shit," she said only half-joking.

The camera resembled a brooch that could be affixed to her purse or worn on her dress.

"Just click right here." He pointed to the small switch on the side.

Rita nodded, pursing her lips. "Pretty neat."

"Let's try it out." He took Rita to stand on the other side of the room. "Okay, go."

She pressed down on the switch. Seconds later, a picture of Jinx appeared on the screen.

Jake grinned.

"I see you do have some skills," Jinx teased.

"Very funny. Now listen, Rita, when you go in there, try to get as many pictures as possible of the inside, any cameras, the metal box layout with the valuables, stuff like that."

"It'll probably be better if I clip it onto my purse. I can get a better angle of stuff that way."

"Right," Jake agreed. He worked with it a little until it was secure on her purse. It looked like a fancy buckle. He stepped back to observe his handiwork. "Ready?"

"Yep."

"Easy does it," Jinx said, giving her a light peck on the lips.

She used the pad of her thumb to wipe away the hint of lipstick on his mouth. She started for the door and then stopped. She turned, frowning. "Where's Eva?"

"Went for a swim."

Rita eyed him for a minute, but Jake wouldn't look at her. "Tell her to meet me at the casino around three. No, scratch that. Xavier will be there, I'm sure. He doesn't need to see me and Eva together. Just tell her to call me so we can hook up later on. I'll have my phone on vibrate, but she can leave me a message."

"Yeah, I'll tell her," Jake said, keeping his attention on the computer screen.

Rita gave him one more look, slashed her eyes in Jinx's direction. Jinx shrugged his shoulders, not knowing any more than she did.

She closed the door behind her.

Jinx meandered over to the bar and poured himself a glass of Coke. He waited awhile, hoping that Jake would open up and spill his guts. The suspense was killing him.

"I know you're waiting for me to say something," Jake blurted.

"Naw, not at all," he lied. "But hey, if you wanna talk . . ."

Jake chuckled, needing a bit of levity in his morning. He spun around in the chair to face his brother.

"Things are pretty bad between me and Eva."

Jinx put his glass down and gave Jake his full attention. "You fucked up, didn't you?"

Jake twisted his lips to the side, ready to protest. "Yeah, big-time."

"Is it about the kid?"

Jake nodded.

Jinx was silent.

"Made me sleep on the couch. That never happened before."

Jinx tried not to laugh. "Damn man, what did you say to the woman?"

"That's just it, I didn't say anything. I didn't respond, re-act, nothing."

Jinx shook his head in disbelief. "You know better than that. I bet she had a fit."

"Pretty much."

"Did you try talking to her this morning?"

He thought about their aborted conversation. "Not really."

"Then you need to talk to her, man. Tell her how you feel and why. She'll understand. Eva is good people, bro, and she loves you."

"It's not that easy."

"Of course it is. She's your wife."

"Naw, you don't understand. See . . ." He reminded Jinx about his confession to Eva regarding their friend Earl and that even though she acted like she understood, she still had him sleeping on the couch, knowing how bad the ship was rocking last night and what that did to him.

"Jake, she was mad. And she had every right to be."

He jumped up. "And I don't? We promised each other: no kids. We agreed. So how did this happen? She did it on purpose, and that's what's really digging at me, man. She tricked me. It's what trifling women do to a brother when they wanna hook 'im. Not to somebody you claim to care about."

"Jake, be for real. Do you honestly believe that Eva is trifling? Come on."

He couldn't answer. It wasn't Eva he was angry with; it was himself.

"You have a chance that a lot of folks don't get."

Jake looked at Jinx. "What's that?"

"The chance to make things right." He reached out and clasped his shoulder. "Right for both of us, with your kid." He waited a beat. "Eva's the best thing that ever happened to you. Don't blow that for what you think might happen. The kid will have her genes too." He gave his brother a crooked smile.

"What if it's a girl?" he asked, trying to imagine a tiny version of Eva.

"Then she'll probably knock you upside the head every time you screw up, just like her mama."

They both rolled with laughter.

"Yeah, man, you're probably right," he said, still chuckling.

"So . . . you gonna talk to her?"

"Yeah." He nodded his head. "I am."

"Tell her the truth. All of it."

26

Rita walked up to the security booth that sat outside the ship's safe. "Good morning."

The security guard, tucked away in a glass booth, looked up from reading a gaming magazine. He took her in all at once, his tongue slowly traveling over his lips.

Rita smiled.

"How can I help you this morning?" He closed the magazine and focused on Rita.

"I wanted to get into my safe deposit box." She looked at his name tag. "Vincent."

His cheeks flushed. "I'll have to see your identification."

"Of course." She opened her purse, careful not to dislodge the camera, and subtly took a picture of the interior of the booth. She pulled out her wallet and took out her driver's license. She handed it to Vincent.

He looked it over, then gave back at her. "This picture does you no justice," he said, his gaze doing another two-step all over her.

"Aren't you sweet."

"I aim to please." He punched in a couple of keys on the computer, stared at the screen for a couple of minutes, then pressed another button. The printer next to him began to whirr, spitting out a blank signature card.

He pushed it through the slot in the glass booth along with a pen. "If you can just sign here." He pointed to the line where her signature went.

Rita pulled the card toward her. Then acting very girly, she asked. "What is this for?"

"I need to verify your signature against what's on file, and it also gives you permission to enter the vault."

"Oh, very thorough." She signed her name.

"Can't be too careful."

"Is this where you're stationed all the time?" She kept her hand on the card and placed her purse on top of the counter, propping it up so that the camera had a perfect view of the interior of his glass booth. She set it to video.

"Yep, this is my post. Eight hours a day."

"Get much business?" she asked, her tone light and airy.

He shrugged. "Some days are more busy than others. Generally it's the high rollers who come back and forth, especially at night."

"Just how safe is my money with so much traffic? I was a bit reluctant to leave it here. I thought it would be safer in my room."

He looked appalled that she would think such a thing.

"The last place you want to leave anything truly valuable is in your room." He lowered his voice to a whisper. "I mean, let's face it—housekeeping has access to your room twenty-four–seven. Who's to say they won't get a case of the sticky fingers? If you know what I mean."

Her eyes widened, feigning alarm. "You mean the staff would actually steal from the guests?"

"It's been known to happen."

"And you say the safe is really the best place."

"Absolutely. We have complete video surveillance, state-of-the-art locks, and a foolproof system that prohibits anyone who is unauthorized inside the vault. I watch the camera right here whenever anyone goes inside."

"I see." She pressed her palm to her chest, drawing his attention to her cleavage. "I feel much better." She frowned for a moment. "I just had a thought. You can see me when I take out my money or jewelry? That's a bit tempting, don't you think?"

"No, I can only see you when you go in. Once inside, you take out your box and go to a private area."

"Oh." She smiled brightly. "Not that I don't trust you, but everyone who sits here is not you."

He blushed. "Well, unless something happens to me, this is my spot for the duration of the trip. We're kind of short-handed."

"That's wonderful. Now I know I'm in good hands." She made sure she got a good image of the card she signed before giving it back.

He took the card and ran it through the scanner. He turned the computer monitor around to face her. "See, here's the signature from the card." He keyed in some code. Rita made sure to capture his every move. "And here is your signature when you signed up for your box in the vault."

The screen flashed, showing that it was a match.

He turned to her, smiling with pride. "See, foolproof."

"All this technology goes right over my head." She laughed. "As long as it works. Right?"

"It does, I can assure you." He processed a card key and pushed it to her through the opening in the Plexiglas, then pressed a button, and the door to the right of him buzzed open. "Come through this door and walk straight down the corridor. Your box number is on the card, and all of the boxes are numbered. Use it the same way you would an ATM card. Once you insert it in your box slot, then it will open. You can take your box to the room that will be on your right."

Rita took the card and stepped through the door. She gave him a finger wave as she passed his glass booth.

Inside the corridor, she held her purse against her chest, letting the camera roll to include each of the boxes that she passed, passing hers intentionally until she'd covered them all, then retraced her steps.

"Oh, here it is," she murmured for his benefit, knowing that she was being watched. She inserted the card, and the door to the box popped open. She took out the metal box and proceeded to the room on her right. She stepped inside and drew the curtain.

She let the camera pan the room, paying special attention to the corners, where surveillance cameras could be hidden, even though Vincent said otherwise. One couldn't be too careful. She opened her box and checked her winnings, staying a reasonable amount of time, and then left. The door buzzed again when she approached. She walked out to the other side.

"Thank you so much, Vincent. Quite impressive. I feel totally confident that my valuables are safe."

"As long as I'm on duty, you have nothing to worry about."

She smiled brightly. "Have a good day. Maybe I'll see you again—off duty." Her brow arched in invitation, matched by a slow smile.

He licked his lips and adjusted his tie. "I get off at ten."

"I'll keep that in mind." She waved again and walked away, being sure to give him a good look at her swaying hips.

"Worked like a charm," Jinx said as he and Jake watched the scenario unfold on their television monitor.

"I'll download all the video and photographs onto the computer and analyze them. Make sure all the bases are covered, and see what flaws are in their system."

"Doesn't seem like there are any," Jinx said.

"Every system has a flaw. It's only a matter of finding it and manipulating it."

"Well if Suarez's stuff isn't in his room, we better find that flaw."

Jake studied the screen. "Yeah," he muttered. "We'd better."

27

Rita headed back to Jake's cabin, taking a circuitous route, hoping to catch a glimpse of Eva somewhere along the way. She was worried about her cousin. It wasn't like Eva to disappear in the middle of a job. It was clear that there was trouble between her and Jake, but they couldn't let that interfere with the job they were there to do.

The whole baby thing was messing with Eva's head, she had to remember. She'd heard all the stories about biological clocks and whatnot, and she supposed that it must have started its countdown with Eva.

Was she really ready to kick the lifestyle they lived to the curb and become someone's mother? Of the two of them, it was true that Eva was more level-headed, more centered. But at the core of them both was the underlying need to live on the edge, take chances, wreak havoc among the unsuspecting—simply because they could.

She rode the escalator up to the next level. But it was more than that, she reasoned. They were both searching for something, something they hoped to recover—their sense of worth. They both judged their own value by what they were able to attain at the expense of others, the same way it had been done to them.

They'd been victimized since they were kids. Now the world was their victim, and any- and everything were up for grabs. Enough was never enough, almost as if what they acquired couldn't fill the void in their souls.

Could Eva really let that all go? Was this baby a substitute to fill the gap—and would it be enough?

She crossed the expanse of the Lido Deck and spotted Xavier in close conversation with a woman. She halted her step, moved to the side to get a better view. She watched as Xavier worked his South American magic.

Her stomach suddenly knotted.

Damn.

She turned and hurried off, going straight to Jake's cabin.

"Where's Eva?" Rita asked the instant she was inside the cabin.

"Why? What's going on?" Jake asked, turning away from the monitor to focus on Rita.

"I just came from the Lido Deck. And Xavier was there."

"And?" Jinx asked.

"He was with some woman."

Jinx's features pinched. "Why should that bother you?"

She turned hot eyes on him. "I'd swear it was that chick that Eva's boss used to date. Whatshername."

"Traci," Jake supplied.

"Right!" She snapped her fingers. "They were very cozy."

"Yeah, Eva told me that she'd run into her on the ship, but she'd ignored her, acted like Traci was talking to the wrong person."

"Traci may be a lot of things, but she's no fool. How long do you think it will be before she runs into Eva again? Then what?"

"We'll deal with it if we must. We all know that Xavier is a ladies' man. And we all know that Traci is a man's lady," Jake said. "They were probably just talking."

"We don't need her in the way. We have enough complications as it is," Rita said.

"Well, we can't worry about that right now. Maybe it's nothing. You don't think you've lost your art of persuasion, do you?" Jake asked.

Rita rocked to the side. "Of course not."

"Then we have nothing to worry about. We go ahead with the plan."

"Yeah, and exactly what is the plan? We have less than a day and a half before the ship docks. We don't know for sure where he's keeping the stash and how we're going to make the switch."

Jake winked. "Jinx and I were working that all out when you busted in."

She pursed her lips. "All I know is, the only bracelets I want around my wrists are diamonds." She sauntered off to the minibar and fixed an early afternoon drink. She turned to them with the drink in her hand. "So how did the pictures come out?"

"Perfect. You did a great job. Here, come take a look." Jake moved over on the bed and pulled up the video on the television screen.

Rita watched in awe. "Wow. That little camera thingy really works."

"As they say in the hood, *I got skillz.*" Jake chuckled.

"Okay, Mr. Brilliant, how do we make the switch? And what if the stuff is in the safe? There's no way to get in there without that card key and signature verification."

"You didn't call me brilliant for nothing."

He laid out the scenario.

Lenora Ingram checked into the motel in Miami. Directly across the street from the airport. In two days, she would be a wealthy woman. The only thing hanging around her neck was her husband. She looked at him as he neatly put his shoes in the closet.

When they first met, those little things were cute, his quirky neatness habits, his enthusiastic but often awkward lovemaking, and even his stutter. Now, she couldn't stand any of it—or him.

She wished she could blame it all on Jerry and their illicit affair. But she couldn't. It rested with her, entirely.

For years she'd had dreams of making her parents proud—as proud of her as they were of her two brothers, both cops, and of her sister, who was the light in her mother's eye, with a minivan full of kids.

Lenora was always in their shadow, from the time they were little kids growing up in the suburbs of Long Island. She was the sickly one, always with one illness or ailment after the other, the one who didn't get the best grades or make the teams or have the handsome basketball captains ringing her doorbell on Friday nights.

Everything for her had been a struggle. A struggle to keep up, to be seen, and her diminutive stature only spotlighted that problem.

It was easy for her to be overlooked, passed over, go

unnoticed. They all laughed when she said that she too was going into the police force.

"Don't be ridiculous," her retired detective father admonished. "The force is no place for you."

"You need to find yourself a good man like your sister and have some kids," her mother said.

Lenora was determined to prove them wrong. First she married Stan to please her parents. But when she discovered that she could never have children, she knew that was yet another disappointment to her folks. So she signed up for the police department against their adamant objections.

She barely made it through the academy, suffering several bouts of bronchitis and a life-threatening case of pneumonia. But she *made* it—only to be relegated to a desk job due to health concerns.

She toughed it out for four years, being the dutiful working wife until she read a bulletin about recruitment for the FBI. Physically it was the best thing to happen to her. The grueling training that she was put through actually helped instead of hindered her health. The increase in pay afforded her the best nutritionist, and through hard work and determination she made it up the ranks to Special Agent with her own staff and responsibilities.

But all her years of scraping and scrapping for attention had molded her into a nail-eating, hard-nosed bitch of a woman. She bloomed when she could crunch her high heel into the back of another. Her cheeks glowed when she solved a case and sent criminals away for the rest of their lives—guilty or not. She had something to prove.

Yet for all her victories within the agency, the very nature of her sex kept her in place. She soon learned she would only go so far standing up.

It was Jerry who opened the door for her in more ways

than one. He not only showed her what great sex was really like, but he repaid her favors with favors of his own—giving her the prime cases and seeing that her pay scale was bumped up regularly.

It was a shame that she'd have to screw over Jerry too.

Lenora took off her high heels and kicked them to the side. She looked for her purse. She was dying for a cigarette.

Stan wrinkled his nose when the first cloud of smoke filled the air. "M-must you?"

He actually has the nerve to look annoyed. "Must I what?" she asked, full of innocence.

"Smoke."

She ignored his question. "You need to go down to the front desk and arrange for a rental car."

"It's already t-taken care of. We can p-pick it up from the rental office in the morning."

"Good." She continued to smoke.

Stan shook his head and went into the bathroom for a quick shower. It was almost ninety degrees, and Lenora had the air-conditioning on low. He was sweating like a bull.

He turned on the water and went over his plan.

A few minutes of peace, Lenora thought as she listened to the water run. She stubbed out her cigarette and stretched across the bed, tossing an arm across her eyes.

Just as she was beginning to relax, her cell phone rang. She jumped up, snatching it off the nightstand. She checked the incoming number.

"Yes."

"I've made contact."

Lenora breathed a sigh. "Good. Just do what you do best, and I'll meet you where we planned."

"You'll have my money, right?"

"Didn't I say that I would? Have I ever gone back on my word?"

"Just checking."

Lenora chuckled. "You are much too paranoid. Everything will be fine. I have them by the short hairs."

"I never would have believed it of Eva."

"Nothing in this life surprises me. You and I are perfect examples of what's possible."

The water in the bathroom shut off. "Gotta go. Keep your eyes open, and let me know the minute anything looks funny."

"I will." Traci hung up the phone. She stood in the walkway for a moment, thinking. What Lenora offered would set her financially straight for quite some time. But she was small potatoes compared to Xavier Suarez. She smiled.

28

The swim had helped to clear her head, although it did nothing for her hairdo. In the poolside dressing room, Eva wrapped a towel around her damp hair and one around her body. Absently she looked down at her stomach. Flat as a board. But that wouldn't last much longer. In a few months, it would grow round, her back would ache, her breasts would swell, and her nose would probably get wide.

She wouldn't be the sexy, curvaceous woman whom she saw in the mirror today. She'd be fat and pregnant.

All her life, her looks and her body had been her ammunition, and she used them at will. How many times had Jake told her that he adored her body, how perfect it was? Would he ever be able to look at her the same way again, with the same hot lust in his eyes?

And what of their love life? She was a sexual woman, needing to get laid as often as she needed to eat. She'd heard the horror stories of couples whose sex life diminished to near zero after having children. Was that what was in store for her and Jake—if they even stayed together?

A chasm of emptiness suddenly opened up inside her. *Not being together with Jake?* The unthinkable rocked her back on her heels. She grabbed the edge of the sink. Jake was everything to her. Everything. She tried to see into a future without him in it, and she couldn't do it. She stared harder into the mirror, and his reflection might as well have been right there beside her own, grinning that sly grin and making her blush like a virgin.

All her life she'd searched for some purpose, some validity to her existence. She'd found it in him and now in the child she carried. She wasn't going to lose either one.

She turned away from the dressing room mirror and hurried out. It was time she got back in the game.

Eva pushed open the door to the cabin.

Jake, Jinx, and Rita jumped in surprise.

"Girl, where have you been?" Rita demanded.

Eva said, "Everybody but Jake Kelly I want out of here right now." Her arm was outstretched toward the open door.

Jinx and Rita looked at each other, then cast furtive glances at Jake as they approached the door.

"You look totally ridiculous giving orders wrapped up in towels," Rita whispered as she crossed the threshold.

Eva made a face, shut the door behind them, drew in a breath, and marched across the room to stand above her husband. "You sit right there and listen to what I have to say," she said, wagging a finger of warning at him. "I want us to get one thing straight Jake Kelly—I love you. I want us to work, and I want this baby." She stomped her foot in punctuation. "Yeah, I know I should have told you I wanted to stop taking the pills, and I didn't. I didn't because I knew what you were going to say. I'm sorry I didn't tell you, but I'm not sorry I'm pregnant with our baby. Ours."

She huffed and began pacing in front of him.

"I know I'm not going to be beautiful and sexy in a couple of months." She turned to him. "But you're not always going to be beautiful and sexy either."

Jake bit back a smile.

"I know it's going to be hard. But we can do it. We can do anything, together. You said so, but only about work: the con, the next job. This is bigger, so much bigger and so much more important than any of that. And maybe, just maybe this baby is what we've been looking for all along—some roots, some sense to this life." She blinked back tears.

"Can I get up now?"

She swallowed over the knot in her throat and slowly nodded her head.

Jake rose and stepped up to her. "When you get fat and ugly, I'll still think about lovin' you." He grinned, and she gave him a tap in the ribs. He moved closer. "When you get old and gray, I'll still love every inch of you." He cupped her cheek in his palm. "This is not about the baby. It's about me and stuff I haven't been able to let go, stuff I believed I would pass on to any kid of mine, and I never wanted to take that chance."

She looked up into his eyes. "What do you mean?"

He took her hand. "Come 'ere, let's sit down and really talk."

They sat side by side on the bed, and Jake poured out his heart, set his fears and his faults at her feet, and hoped that she wouldn't crush them.

"My father was a beast of a man: cold, brutal, and distant. He thought beating your ass on a regular basis was good parenting. Said it would make me and my brother men." He laughed harshly and shook his head. "And my mother after taking her own beatings would tell me, 'You're just like your father.'"

Eva listened, seeing a part of her husband she'd never known. Sure, she understood that he'd had a hard life. They both had. And each of them had found ways to deal with those internal scars. But what she did not know, until now, was how deeply Jake was scarred. His wounds were so deep and emotionally debilitating that it left him unable to separate himself from the man who abused him.

". . . and it scares me . . . that I might be just like him."

Dark shadows moved across his eyes as he stared off into a past that was never completely behind him.

Eva took his hand. "Look at me."

Slowly he raised his gaze and looked into her eyes.

"Fuck him," she said simply.

A flicker of confusion then mild amusement skipped across Jake's features. It would take Eva to break it down to the bare basics.

He snapped his fingers. "Just like that, huh?"

"Yeah." She popped her fingers too. "Just like that." She leaned in. "Your father was a bastard, and I'm sure he's rotting in hell, but you survived it. You may not be a model citizen, but you survived. That has to mean something."

"Are you sure you're ready for this? Our lives will be changed forever."

Eva smiled. "I have no idea, but I want to try."

"I guess if we can get away with the stuff we've pulled over the years, raising a kid should be a piece of cake."

She pulled the towel from her head then the one

wrapped around her body. "I hear that pregnant women have the best orgasms."

"Is that right?" he murmured, leaning close to nibble at her ear.

She sighed. "So I hear."

"Why don't we check it out for ourselves? Just to be sure."

"Yeah," she purred as his mouth teased a nipple. "Why don't we?"

Eva and Jake lay curled in bed together, simmering from the afterglow. Jake tenderly stroked her spine, feeling her warm breath brush against his chest.

Eva had stood by him at every turn, even when she disagreed. The more he thought it out, the more he realized that the only way to let go of the past was to take a step into the future. That's what he intended to do.

He was going to get them out of this mess and start over, start fresh. He smiled as Eva nestled closer. They would certainly have some stories to tell their kid when it grew up. But who would ever believe them?

Eva walked around the compact cabin while Jake outlined the updated plan. She nodded in agreement as she paced.

"I think you need to stay as low-key as possible with Traci wandering around," Jake added once he'd finished with the scenario.

Eva twisted toward him. "I need to be there. Part of this whole plan was my idea too. I'm not going to let that . . . woman interfere. I'll just deal with her."

"Do you think she may have called Sebastian?"

"It crossed my mind," she said, a furrow of concern inching across her brow. "But she and Sebastian didn't part on the best of terms. She'd really have to come up with a doozy of a reason to call him."

"What if she does?"

She twisted her lips in thought. "I'll think of something."

A cell phone rang. They both went for their phones. It was Eva's.

She looked across at Jake, her eyes wide with alarm. "Sebastian," she mouthed.

"Sooner's come rather than later."

Eva pressed the XW icon on the phone.

"Hello?"

"Eva, it's Sebastian."

"Hey, Bass. How are you?"

"Not so good. When will you be coming back? I know you said about a week. But we have some discrepancies with the inventory."

Her heart slowed. At least that was something she could deal with.

"What kind of discrepancy?"

"We got a call today from our supplier in Hong Kong. They were asking did we get the double shipment that you ordered and wanted to know when they would be paid. I have no idea what they are talking about, and there are no records of any recent shipments from Hong Kong."

The ship suddenly gave off a loud horn blast.

"What in the world was that? Sounded like the horn from hell."

Eva chuckled nervously. "Oh, uh, I have the television on. The uh, History Channel. Anyway, I'll take care of all that as soon as I get back. It's obvious that they must be mistaken."

"Hmmm. I certainly hope so. Because if I find out that someone on this staff is lining their pockets, heads will roll all up and down Seventh Avenue."

"How is everything else going with the line?"

"Hectic, to say the least. You are definitely missed. And it's getting harder for me to be in two places at one time. Your cousin picked a fine time to get ill. How is she, by the way?"

"Coming along day by day. Thanks for asking. Have you found another architect?"

"I'm still interviewing and paying rent on a space that I can't use. It's really draining the budget."

"You'll find someone, and all of this will be a forgotten headache in no time."

"From your lips."

She could hear the noises of the studio in the background and could pretty much see the chaos and comings and goings of the designers. She had a moment of nostalgia. Quiet as it was kept, she really liked her job. She liked the normalcy of that part of her life. She would miss it dearly.

"I should let you get back to being Florence Nightingale, although it is beyond my capabilities to see you in that role."

Eva laughed. "You take care, Bass, and I'll see you soon."

"You do the same and give my regards to Rita."

"I sure will. Bye."

She disconnected the call.

"Well?"

"So far, Traci hasn't called, but the order that I placed for the zirconia for this gig of ours popped up. I really didn't think the vendors would call."

Jake chewed on his thumbnail. "He can't get into your computer, can he?"

She shook her head. "No. Thank God it's password protected. I was holding my breath, thinking he might ask me for the code."

"Small favors," he murmured. "There's not much you can do about it from here."

"True." She plopped down in the chair by the bed. "I really feel bad about leaving Bass in the lurch like this. Things are so tough for him right now."

"It's not your fault."

"At least if I was there . . . maybe I could help. If he can't get the financing he needs, he may actually lose the business."

"Is it that bad?"

She nodded.

They were silent for a moment, each caught up in their private thoughts.

Jake snapped his fingers and looked at Eva. A slow smile crept across her mouth as she watched the wheels spin in his head.

29

Rita wandered around the casino until she found an empty seat at the roulette table. Games of chance weren't really her thing, but she'd give it a shot.

She hadn't seen Xavier since earlier that morning, and there were no messages from him on her phone either. That worried her. It was imperative that she gain access to his room, and she couldn't very well do that if someone else was beating her time, namely Traci Jennings.

She placed her bet and watched the wheel spin.

"I didn't think this was your kind of game," a voice from behind her whispered.

She glanced over her shoulder. "Well, hello. I'd given you up."

"Never." Xavier glanced at the roulette wheel. "I have been very busy. Things that needed to be taken care of before we dock in Miami."

"I see."

"Would you care to join me for a drink . . . before dinner?"

"I would. Thank you. I wasn't doing very well over here anyway. And being in your company is just the thing to lift my spirits."

He took her elbow. "Come. I have a table reserved." He escorted her to the top deck of the ship to the glass-enclosed restaurant. They were quickly shown to their table.

Rita looked out onto the calm seas and the ink-black sky dotted with millions of tiny stars.

"This is beautiful. I didn't realize there was a restaurant up here."

Xavier smiled. "I told you: it is my responsibility to please a lovely lady such as you."

Rita actually blushed. "You always know what to say."

"If only I did." His expression grew serious. "I've been thinking a lot of you."

She reached for the goblet of water. Light danced off its polished surface, making the glass opalescent. "Have you? Is that a good thing?"

"It depends."

"On what?"

"On your answer to my proposition."

"Oh?" Her brows arched over widened eyes of curiosity.

He steepled his fingers beneath his mouth. "I have important business in Miami. It will take several days. I have a home there."

Her pulse quickened.

"I'm inviting you to stay as my guest while I am in Miami."

She lowered her lids and toyed with her glass. "A guest? What kind of guest?"

He smiled at the loaded question. "The kind who bene-fits from my benevolence."

"A guest with benefits—interesting concept."

"It will give us a chance to get to know each other. And then"—he shrugged slightly—"who knows."

"Do you want an answer now?"

"After we eat, after you come to my suite and share my bed. Then you can decide."

A hot flush raced straight to her head and pounded against her temples. Her underarms grew damp. She reached for the water and then changed her mind.

"You seem to have this all figured out," she said, strug-gling to maintain calm in her voice while her thoughts raced.

"Everything in my life is carefully planned. Something you will learn, should you take me up on my offer of hospi-tality."

Her throat had gone so dry, she thought she'd choke if she tried to swallow. This time the goblet of water made it to her lips. She took a long slow drink. This may be her last chance to get into his room, but were they ready? Jake swore up and down that it could be pulled off. But the plan was for *tomorrow,* not tonight. She needed to be sure that everything and everyone was in place.

"Let's order, have a wonderful dinner, an exquisite time in your bed . . . and *if* you are as benevolent as you say, I just might take you up on your offer to be a guest with ben-efits." She smiled wickedly over the rim of her glass.

Xavier tossed his dark head back and laughed from deep in his belly. "As they say in the States . . . You're on." He signaled for the waiter.

After dinner of penne pasta with clam sauce, steamed

mussels, and a garden salad to die for, they danced under the stars and laughed over several glasses of wine.

Rita couldn't remember the last time she'd been romanced or, better yet, seduced. At times when she listened to Xavier tell ribald stories of his life in South America, she was hard-pressed to see him as the ruthless killer and smuggler that he was reported to be. Under the stars and the glow of good food and wine, he was simply a devastatingly handsome, sexy, and charming man.

What would life be like with a man such as Xavier Suarez? She would certainly have all the money and luxuries her heart desired. She'd never have to work a con again. She'd never have to forge documents for extra cash to feed her lust for the finer things in life or concern herself with the trivialities of everyday living. She would finally be queen of a castle and have a powerful and sinfully wealthy man as her protector. What if everyone was wrong about him?

"You've come a long way from the back streets of Venezuela and Brazil," Rita said as they danced to a slow song.

He held her close, and she inhaled his manly fragrance. She let her eyes drift closed.

"I've worked hard for all that I have attained. I knew since a little boy that I would not grow up in poverty, living forever in a shack with mud for floors."

She heard the underlying pain mixed with determination in his voice.

"What about your family?"

"I take good care of my family. All of them. The money that I make goes back to the town in which I grew up. They have schools now and a small clinic that helps many."

"Not many people would do that. Most would want to get as far away from their pasts as they could." She thought of herself and Eva, always running, always seeking.

"I am not like anyone you have ever known." He leaned back and looked into her upturned face. "Always remember that." He kissed the top of her head and finished the dance. He took her back to their table. "Would you like dessert before we leave?"

Her heart jumped in her chest. "No. Actually, I want to freshen up a bit." She rose and so did he. "I'll be just a minute, and then we can go."

He nodded and watched her as she headed off to the restroom.

Rita pushed the restroom door open, checked all the stalls before taking out her cell phone.

Jake picked up on the second ring. "Yeah . . ."

"It has to be tonight. . . ."

"Tonight!" Eva sputtered. "Are we ready?"

"We have to be. Not much of a choice. We needed Rita to gain access to his room, and tonight is the night. We may not get another chance."

Eva paced with her fist pressed to her lips. "Okay, then we have to get busy. But what about the safe?"

"I'm hoping that everything we need is in the suitcase. If not, we have one more day."

Eva sighed. "Okay. Call Jinx and tell him to bring the bag. And I'll get ready."

"Rita will call us as soon as everything is set on her end."

Jinx arrived shortly with the bag. "She's with him now?" he asked as he set the bag down in the center of the room.

"Yeah," Jake said, and went over the information on the computer.

Jinx grumbled something incoherent. Eva flashed him a look. "Rita will be fine. For what it's worth, she's a professional."

There was something about the way she'd looked at Suarez, in a way she'd never looked at him—almost with longing. And it worried Jinx more than he was willing to admit out loud.

"I'm going to get dressed," Eva said, and left the room.

Jake turned to his brother. "I know what you're thinking. Don't."

Jinx wandered aimlessly around the cabin. "I just have a bad feeling about Rita and this guy. You haven't seen them together, I have."

"She's doing her job, Jinx. That's it. When this is over, we'll all walk away, and Rita will too."

"I don't know, man." He shook his head. "I really don't."

Jake studied his brother's worried profile. He knew how much Jinx cared about Rita, how much he always had. But Rita was a wild card. Sure she probably had a soft spot in her heart for Jinx, but Rita—even more so than Eva—was always out for the next big score. And this time Xavier Suarez just might be the jackpot for her. He hoped not. If Rita pulled a fast one on Jinx, he was pretty sure it would do his brother in.

Rita took a last check of her makeup in the bathroom mirror, applied a bit more powder to her nose, and freshened her lipstick. She made sure the vial was tucked deep inside her purse and then shut it.

She looked at her reflection. Would a night with Xavier be everything that she imagined? And what about the morning after? But if she did what she was supposed to do, she'd never find out.

That was the dilemma that plagued her. She turned away from the image of accusation in the mirror and returned to the table.

Whatever happened between her and Xavier would happen. She'd be sure to hold up her end of the arrangement for everyone else's sake. Other than that—the chips would simply have to fall.

30

Rita stepped out of the restroom and was on her way back to her table when she spotted Traci crossing the room in the direction of Xavier. She stood off to the side, out of sight.

Always the gentleman, Xavier rose when Traci approached. His two bodyguards who'd remained unobtrusive during the evening stood as well. The diners seemed not to notice the scene unfolding in front of them.

Traci at first seemed to be cooing and cajoling, while Xavier's expression remained amiable. Rita wasn't sure what Traci said, but Xavier raised his right hand, ever so slightly, and the two men approached. Traci looked from one to the other as they came up on either side of her. Her voice rose as she snatched her arm away from the first man.

Xavier sat down as if nothing out of the ordinary was transpiring in front of him and continued to drink his coffee.

With the speed of a ninja, Traci reached for the table, snatched up Rita's half-filled glass of water, and tossed the contents at Xavier. He barely moved. Rita's heart stopped, expecting a scene right out of *The Sopranos* to jump off.

Xavier picked up the linen napkin and casually wiped the streaks of water from his face and the front of his jacket. His lips barely moved as he said something to the men, but Rita saw something in his eyes that was a first cousin to pure evil. A chill hardened her nipples.

The two guards securely took both of Traci's arms and removed her from the restaurant. The music continued to play; the revelers continued to eat and make merry with hardly an eye turned toward what had just taken place.

Rita's legs felt weak, but she certainly couldn't continue to stand there, and she didn't want to even imagine what was happening to Traci.

She put on her best face and returned to the table. "Sorry I took so long," she said, settling into her seat.

Xavier got up and pulled her chair out without a word.

She sat opposite him, watching his jaw clench and un-clench, the coiled fury held at bay only through sheer will.

"Is everything okay?"

Dark, almost empty eyes looked at her. "Yes. Every-thing is taken care of."

She didn't want to entertain the thought of what that meant.

The corners of his mouth lifted ever so slightly. "If you are ready, we can leave now."

"Sure."

He stood up and came around to help her rise from her seat. He put his large hand at the small of her back and ush-ered her out of the restaurant.

Eva, dressed in the employee uniform, worked her way through the levels, keeping her eyes peeled for an appearance of Traci, while still attempting to look busy. With a passenger load of more than two thousand and two-hundred-plus employees, it was easy to blend in.

She was about to step on the escalator when she caught a glimpse of Traci being walked down the corridor by the two men she'd swear were Suarez's bodyguards. She kept an eye on them until they turned down another hallway and were gone from her line of sight.

What is that about?

She continued up the escalator. When she reached the next level, she took her PDA out of her pocket and pulled up the ship plan on the screen. She scrolled around until she found the location she needed. She turned left, went up one more level, walked down an *Employees Only* corridor, and found the master kitchen. She pushed through the swinging doors as if this was where she belonged.

The kitchen was bustling with activity. The chef blasted out orders to the cooks, steam rose from pots and gave the air a misty look, waiters darted back and forth, bringing orders and taking them out.

She quickly scanned the area until she found what she was looking for. No one paid her any attention when she pulled one of the large service carts out of the swinging doors. It was much heavier than she thought, even with wheels.

"I got it," she said into her headset.

"Good. Come on back until we're ready," Jake responded.

"Any word from Rita?"

"No."

Eva didn't like that. She knew her cousin too well. She didn't like it at all.

"Please, make yourself comfortable," Xavier said once they were inside his cabin. He took off his jacket and tossed it on the couch. "Can I fix you a drink?"

"That would be nice." She followed him over to the bar, thinking of the vial in her purse. From what Eva told her, the stuff worked in about fifteen minutes. All she had to do was slip it into his drink. This could all be over shortly.

He turned to her with a drink in his hand. She took it with her thanks.

"Come, join me over here." He walked over to the couch and sat down. Rita sat next to him.

He studied her for a moment. "What would make a woman like you interested in a man like me?"

The question caught her off guard. She stumbled for an answer. "What do you mean?"

"I can tell you are a very bright woman. And smart women see things, understand things, as do smart men."

Her heart began to hammer in her chest. *Where is this going?* She took a sip of her drink.

"I have a very strong feeling, being a smart man, that you know I am no simple businessman."

The wine sat on the top of her stomach like a brick.

Pull yourself together. Think. She turned her body to better face him. "I know that no simple businessman needs three bodyguards on a cruise ship, if that's what you mean."

He chuckled. "You see, you are a smart woman. I like that." He stroked her cheek with the tip of his finger.

"I need a smart woman. A woman who is unafraid, who is daring."

She listened.

"If I could find that kind of woman to be by my side, I could make her very happy."

Rita licked her lips.

"Many have tried. And I have held many auditions." He smiled at his own joke. "And all have failed. So"—he shrugged—"I continue to search." His eyes rested on her face. "This is your audition. If you pass . . . well, there will be nothing out of your reach."

Her lungs refused to fill with air. Her breaths were short and choppy.

Xavier ran his finger from her chin, down her throat, to the top of her breasts, dipping it teasingly beneath the scoop of her sequined gown.

Rita moaned softly.

Xavier slid one strap off her right shoulder and then her left. "Stand up," he said, his voice thick and urgent.

Rita did as she was told.

"Take it off."

Rita slowly pushed the top of the dress down, the clingy fabric moving like silk across her body, exposing her bare flesh. She pushed the gown over her hips, let it drop to the floor. She stepped over it.

"You are as beautiful as I imagined." His eyes licked across her naked body. Rita shivered.

He reached out and caressed the perfect dark triangle between her legs.

"Open them."

She spread her legs and gasped with startled pleasure when his mouth sampled her offering.

Xavier eased back and looked up at her; a smile heated

the fire in his eyes. Slowly he stood up. "Yes, just as I thought." His lips met hers in a slow, seductive kiss that made her weak. His lips and tongue played with her mouth, teasing and taunting, only hinting at what it could offer until she was shaking with need.

She pulled him to her, her fingers threading through his hair.

With hands that suddenly felt like steel, he grabbed her wrists and pulled her hands away, locking them down at her sides. He shook his head slowly. "Not yet," he murmured. "Come." He led her into his bedroom and shut the door.

Eva returned to the cabin with the service cart.

"Anything?" she asked as she parked the cart in the corner.

"No, not yet," Jake said. He shot a look in Jinx's direction then back at Eva.

Jinx was nursing a drink. He stubbed out his cigarette and stared off into space.

Eva approached Jinx. "You cool?"

He turned and looked at her. "Would you be if it was Jake and some woman you knew he had the hots for?"

"Come on, man," Jake said. "Rita's there to take care of business. You gotta keep your head screwed on straight. Focus."

The ship's horn suddenly blared three long hard blasts.

They all looked at each other.

Hurried footsteps could be heard in the hallway.

"What the—?" Jake jumped up and went to the door. He pulled it open and looked out into the hallway. Several crewmen were donning life jackets.

"Hey," Jake shouted to one of the men running past. "What's going on?"

"A passenger claims they saw someone fall into the water."

Eva flinched, remembering Traci and Suarez's men.

Jake frowned and shut the door.

"I think it may have been Traci," Eva said as the scene ran through her mind once again. She told them what she'd witnessed.

"Damn," Jinx muttered; then his eyes widened. "If Suarez even thinks something is wrong . . . what if—?"

"Don't even go there," Eva warned. "Rita can take care of herself." She flashed a look at Jake.

They all sat in a tight silence, waiting for the call.

Xavier's hard, driving thrusts filled her to near bursting. She was sure he would break her in half, and she devoured every minute of it, giving back everything she got.

Her head spun with pleasure. His hands were everywhere at once it seemed, and his mouth was relentless in its pursuit to explore every square inch of her searing flesh.

He whispered and groaned in his native tongue, the lush language only adding to the flames that were building in her stomach.

Rita never had a man like him. Never felt like this before. She knew she wanted it again and again and that frightened her more than the unspeakable climax that exploded in a million little pieces inside her.

Rita listened to Xavier's heavy breathing beside her. Her body still shuddered in unexpected spasms of delight.

The bedside phone rang. Its sound was piercing in the silence of the dimly lit bedroom.

Xavier muttered a curse and reached for the phone. He listened for several moments.

"Good. Stay in your room. And do not disturb me until morning." He hung up and rolled onto his side so that he pressed against Rita's back. He kissed her spine. She shivered.

His hand stroked her hips, then pulled her roughly against him, his erection demanding attention.

"Your audition is not finished," he breathed hot against her neck. He raised her leg over his hip and pushed deep inside her with a grunt that ended in a hiss.

Rita muffled her scream deep in the overstuffed pillow as bright lights went off inside her head and her body burned from the assault.

Weak and shaky, Rita eased from the bed to the sound of Xavier's gentle snores. She tiptoed into the bathroom and quietly shut the door. She turned on the light and was stunned by her reflection.

All along the cords of her neck her light honey complexion reflected the beginnings of purple bruises from his suckling. They ran a trail from her neck down to the rise of her breasts.

She looked down. On the inside of her thighs were imprints from his hands from when he held her legs wide apart.

Rita shut her eyes, and a shiver ran through her. How could she ever explain this to Jinx? Even more, how would she ever be so satisfied ever again without Xavier?

She couldn't.

She turned on the water, grabbed a washcloth from the rack above the sink, and pressed cold water against the marks that she knew would take days to disappear. With hot water she cleaned herself, washing away the sticky residue.

With shaky hands, she turned off the water and once again looked at herself in the mirror. She couldn't stand what she saw. She turned off the light and returned to the bedroom.

Xavier was still soundly asleep. She went into the living room where she'd left her purse. It was nearly eleven. She took the vial from her purse and poured the contents into one glass then filled it with wine. She gently shook the glass. She drew in a breath and filled another glass with wine then returned to the bedroom. She put Xavier's glass on the nightstand on his side, then went around and crawled back into bed.

Xavier stirred, reached out, and cupped her tender left breast. "Open your legs for me," he said in a rough whisper.

He climbed on top of her, lifted her legs over his shoulders, and rode her until she screamed in release.

Propped up against the mound of pillows, they sipped their wine. Rita's heart raced with every swallow that he took. Suppose it didn't work?

"Tomorrow morning we dock in Miami," he said. He finished off his wine and put it down. "Have you decided?"

She turned to him and smiled. "Are you sure you still want me as your guest?"

"I am a man who always knows what he wants," he said, each word coming out slower than the last. He frowned as the effects of the drug began to kick in. He tried to stand but failed. His eyes rolled for a moment in their sockets. He chuckled, struggling against the inevitable. He turned his head toward her in slow motion. "There was no need to drug me. . . . I would have given you anything . . . you wanted." His face twisted into an ugly mask. He awkwardly lunged toward her, his large hands finding her neck. She kicked and fought, gasping for air as his grip tightened.

Then just as suddenly as the attack began, it stopped, and he slumped against the pillows.

Rita sucked in air, coughing and choking as she stumbled from the bed. She tripped her way into the living room and called the cabin. "Now," she choked out. Tears ran down her cheeks.

She grabbed her clothes and quickly put them on, looked around the entire suite for any traces of her. She took the glass she'd used and stuck it in her purse. She ran into the bathroom and grabbed up the towel and washcloth, balling them both up.

Pulling herself together, she went back into the bedroom. Xavier was out cold. Her throat knotted. She went to the bed and leaned over him.

"I'm sorry," she whispered. "I wish things could have been different."

The knock on the door jerked her upright.

"Room service."

She'd expected to hear Eva's voice. She tossed one last look at Xavier from over her shoulder and went to the door.

Jinx stood on the other side. He took one look at her, and shame filled her.

He brushed by her. "Let's get this over with." He pushed the service cart into the suite. "Get the suitcase."

She went to the closet and pulled out the suitcase.

Jinx called Jake on the phone. "We have the case."

"Good. Hang on." He brought the impression of the suitcase up on the computer screen. "I'm going to input the combination into your PDA."

Jinx waited, watching Rita from the corner of his eyes while she sat in stony silence in a chair by the window of the bedroom.

His PDA beeped. He went to the suitcase and put in a series of numbers and letters. He pulled the latch. It didn't open.

"Shit." A line of perspiration broke out across his forehead.

Xavier groaned.

They both looked at him. Jinx tried again.

This time it opened to a case filled with hundred-dollar bills, but no diamonds.

Rita hurried over to the service cart, removed the bucket of ice, and lifted the linen tablecloth. The counterfeit money that she'd spent weeks in creating sat in even rows.

They quickly made the switch, leaving the top row with the real money and the fake underneath, locked the suitcase, and returned it to the closet.

"You can't very well go to the safe looking like you've just been fucked," Jinx ground out.

Rita winced, drew herself up. "I'll go back to the suite and change," she said quietly. "Let's go."

She crawled beneath the cart onto the bottom tray and curled into a tight ball.

Jinx pulled the sides of the table down and dropped the tablecloth over it. He checked all around to be sure Rita couldn't be seen.

Gritting his teeth, he pushed the heavy load out the door and into the hallway.

31

Jinx and Rita returned to the cabin. Eva took one look at her cousin and knew the worst had happened. She didn't even want to know what was going on in Jinx's head.

"I'm going to my room to change," Rita said softly.

"I'll go with you," Eva said.

Jake looked up but held his tongue.

The instant they were in Rita's cabin, Eva jumped on her. "Tell me what I think happened didn't."

Rita kept her back to her cousin.

"Rita . . . Oh, God. Why? All you were supposed to do was fix his drink."

"I know. I know." She turned to Eva. "He's . . . not what you think."

"Not what I think! Have you lost your mind? He's a

murderer, for godsake. And if I'm not mistaken, he's had Traci disposed of." She told Rita about what had happened earlier.

Rita's insides sank. She could still see Traci being carted off by those two well-dressed goons.

"You don't know that for sure."

"Maybe not. But one thing I do know is that you hurt Jinx to no end."

"Since when did you give a damn about Jinx's feelings?"

"Since I realized that . . . men have feelings too, Rita. That they hurt too, have wants and needs and secrets too." She slowly approached Rita, who looked like she wanted to run. "Just like me and you. We've been running and searching for something all of our lives, and it's been right in front of us for a long time. But we've been so busy looking for the next best thing, we couldn't see it."

Tears filled Rita's eyes. "Jinx can't really want me. He can't really want me, 'cause at the heart of him with all his faults and quirks, he's a good guy—and good guys don't go for women like me."

"But he has gone for a woman like you." She reached out and wiped the tears away. "And it's about time you started thinking of yourself as someone worthy of being loved and not used."

Rita hung her head. "It's probably too late now."

"One thing I've discovered on this little excursion is that it's never too late." She paused for a beat. "Now come on. We have some diamonds to lift."

Rita put the stash of zirconia in her oversize pocketbook. "Sure looks like the real thing," she muttered as she closed the pocketbook.

Jake handed her the encoded card key for Xavier's box. "This should work."

"Should?" Rita said.

"It will. Trust me."

"Get in and out of there as quickly as possible," Eva said. "I'll be nearby just in case anything goes wrong."

Rita nodded. She looked at Jinx. He flexed his jaw and turned away.

Eva followed her out.

When Rita arrived at the security desk, she cringed when she realized that the young man she'd flirted with was not on duty.

She turned left and headed toward the noisy casino.

Eva frowned. Moments later, Rita's voice came through her headset.

"You're going to have to cause some kind of diversion," she whispered into the tiny microphone attached to her bra.

"Why? What's wrong?"

"There's a different guy at the desk. The cameras are going to see that I'm not opening my box."

"Shit. Okay. I'll think of something. Just go ahead."

Rita went back to the security desk. "Hi. I need to get into my box." She smiled. He ignored it.

"ID."

She went in her bag and pulled out her identification and slid it through the small opening.

He looked it over then at her. "Card key."

She handed that to him as well. He slid it through a slot next to the computer, and a signature card spit out of the printer. He pushed it through the slot.

"Sign at the X."

She did as instructed. "Busy night, huh?"

He muttered something she couldn't understand.

Her signature approval popped up on the screen. The side door beeped open, and she stepped through.

Rita walked down the narrow walkway, passing the boxes. Xavier's was next. All she could do was pray that whatever Eva had in mind worked.

She took the card key and slid it in. The door to the box popped open without a hitch.

She held her breath, waiting for alarms to go off. She took the metal box out and went into the private room. She pulled the curtain.

Pulling the bag of zirconias from her purse, she made the transfer, leaving enough of the real thing in the box as instructed.

Drawing in a breath, she stuck her stash down in her purse, closed the box, and returned it.

Her heart was beating a mile a minute as she walked back to the door.

She saw Eva through the Plexiglas partition chatting amiably with the surly guard.

She knocked on the glass to get his attention. The door buzzed.

"Thanks and good night." She gave him a finger wave and walked away.

Her legs felt like spaghetti, and she was sure that at any moment a big grubby hand was going to clamp down on her shoulder and drag her away for eternity.

She collapsed in relief when she finally made it back to the cabin.

Jake was beaming. "Good job."

"It ain't over yet. We still have to get off this ship," Jinx said. "How long is loverboy going to be out?"

Rita grimaced.

"At least twelve hours. Stuff works like a charm," Jake said from experience.

Moments later, Eva arrived. "Close one," she breathed, shutting the door behind her.

"What did you say to that guy anyway?" Rita asked.

"I started talking about the alleged person who went overboard. Told him how scary it was and whatnot. He said it was probably somebody throwing trash over the side. Said it happens all the time."

"At least it kept him busy and his eyes off the monitors. By the time they play the tapes back, we'll be long gone," Jake said.

"We need to get everything packed up. I have some calls to make to my connections in Miami, make sure we're all set." Jinx got up from his seat. Rita approached.

"John."

She rarely used his first name, Jinx thought, the sound of it softening the iron ball in his gut. He drew in air through his nose.

"Yeah," he muttered, keeping his attention focused on packing up the equipment.

"Can we talk? Later?"

Jinx turned his head and looked up at her. He tried to see her without Suarez's hands all over the body he loved, Suarez's mouth on places that should be reserved only for him . . . He blinked away the vision. "Not sure what there is to talk about, Rita," he said, the words falling like snow between them, soft but cold.

She turned away and ran into Eva's stare. *Talk to him,* she mouthed.

Rita squeezed her eyes shut and shook her head.

Eva pursed her lips into a tight pout, crossed the room

in two steps, and grabbed Rita by the arm, practically lifting her off her feet. She dragged her back to Jinx's side.

His head snapped up.

"Look, we all make mistakes," Eva said, looking from one to the other. "And there is no one in this room with a clean enough slate to throw stones. We all got dirty, stinking laundry. But the bottom line is we're . . . family. We love each other. You two love each other," she said, flicking her index finger back and forth between Jinx and Rita, "and we two love each other," she added hooking her thumb over her shoulder at Jake. She huffed.

Jake stepped up and put his arm around Eva's waist. "We've been in the game too long, bro. When you're in it too long, you begin to believe your own con." He reached toward Jinx. "We just get caught up, man."

Jinx lowered his head. He ran his tongue across his lips. "You wanna help me with this stuff or just stand there?" he asked, looking up at Rita.

Rita felt as if she would burst with relief. She blinked back tears and sat next to him on the small couch. She started wrapping up the wires. He may not be as dashing and insatiable as Xavier Suarez, she thought. But he loved her, and he wanted her in his life with no strings attached. All he wanted was for her to love him back. Her hand brushed his as they both reached for the next cable. She looked into his eyes. Yeah, she could do that.

Eva grinned and turned to Jake. She angled her head to the side. "So now you're a relationship counselor too, huh?"

"I call 'em like I see 'em." He winked. "You ain't too bad yourself."

She tugged his belt and pulled him to her. "I think I'm going to have to check out your credentials . . . later."

He leaned down and pecked her lightly on the lips. "Strip search?" He put his hands on her waist.

"Uh, I think there's something I need to tell you all." Rita stood and instinctively smoothed her blouse.

"What?" Eva and Jake echoed.

Rita glanced over at Jinx. She walked to the center of the room. "Before . . . Xav . . . Suarez passed out." She swallowed. "He realized he was being drugged. He tried to fight it. He . . . tried to kill me."

"What!" Jinx jumped up from the couch. He came over and grabbed her arms, letting his eyes run over her. "What did he do to you?" he asked in a tone so chilling, it stiffened her spine.

She took the scarf from around her neck.

Eva gasped at the ugly bruises that circled Rita's neck like a choker. But were they the result of an attack or . . .

The cords in Jinx's neck tightened, rising above the muscles beneath as if pulled by an invisible string. He picked up a glass from the table and hurled it across the room in helpless frustration.

Jinx paced the room like a man possessed, hurling curses and threats. Pleas to settle down fell on deaf ears. He wanted to hurt Suarez, make him pay for hurting Rita. He'd been so ready to accuse her of sleeping with Suarez, and she'd been fighting for her life. He never even gave her a chance to explain. His shame slowly tempered his anger.

He looked at Rita, and the thought that he could have lost her sucked the air out of his chest. And for what? For some crooked FBI agent whose hands were far dirtier than theirs.

Jinx ran his palm across his head and exhaled. "Let's get this bastard."

"That's the plan," Jake said in all seriousness.

Jinx walked up to Rita. His mouth tried to form words to apologize for thinking the worst, but nothing came out. He took her hand. "Let's go. We need a good night's sleep."

As Rita lay next to Jinx in the comfort of darkness, a part of her hated that she led Jinx to believe that nothing happened between her and Suarez, that the bruises were all a result of her fighting for her life. But it was best this way. It was an episode of her life that she would tuck away out of Jinx's reach. He need never know. Only she would.

She closed her eyes, and images of her and Xavier taunted her throughout the night.

32

Jake checked his watch. "The ship should be docking in about a half hour."

"You think the drug is still working¿" Rita asked, clenching and unclenching her hands as she sat on the very edge of the chair.

"Usually twelve hours, give or take thirty minutes," Eva responded.

"But we aren't taking any chances," Jake said. "You need to change your look totally. We can't risk either Suarez or one of his boys recognizing you."

"My thought exactly," Rita said. She took a curly honey-brown wig from the bag and set it on the table. "And just to be sure." She stood and put a small pillow on her stomach and secured it with a thin belt, then lowered her billowy flowered top. She grinned at the effect. "They won't be looking for a pregnant woman with curly brown hair."

Eva absently placed her hand on her stomach. She'd actually look like that in a few months. A moment of panic seized her. What was she thinking? She was not mother material. She'd never had anyone to emulate, had no idea how to care about anyone other than herself—and maybe Jake, but he was grown.

Jake put his arm around her shoulder.

"It's gonna be all right," he said only to her. "I don't have a clue either."

She looked up into his easy smile. He always could read her like a book. "The blind leading the blind, huh?"

"Happens all the time." He kissed the tip of her nose. "Let's get busy."

When they emerged from the cabin, the ship was a bevy of activity. People swarmed the walkways, and crew members raced around, helping with luggage and directions.

"Stay together," Jake said, "and keep your eyes open. We need to be one of the first off this ship."

They made the slow trek to the front of the ship, where they would disembark.

The ship rocked as it approached the dock. Eva squeezed Jake's hand. He looked down at her and winked.

Then behind them was some commotion and pushing.

Jake looked over his shoulder. It was Suarez's two bodyguards. They were shoving their way to the front.

"Oh, damn," Rita whispered, and then put on a pair of sunglasses.

Grumbles and startled curses rose up and down as passengers were pushed and shoved aside. The two men cut a path between bodies.

"Just be cool," Jake urged. "We're almost there."

The gangway opened just as the two men reached the front and practically assaulted the captain, who was at the ready to say his good-byes and thanks to the departing passengers.

They started shouting in Spanish and gesturing, their tanned faces flushed with anger.

"They must have found Suarez," Eva whispered to Jake.

"Yeah."

The captain raised his hand, signaling for assistance. Deep creases etched themselves into his forehead, and he listened to the men. Two white-uniformed crew members forced their way through the tight knot of people.

There were a good two hundred people in front of Jake, Eva, Jinx, and Rita.

"Damn, what if he's dead?" Rita whispered.

"He better not be. They'll hold everyone on the ship," Jake said. He peered over heads to try to get a look at what was happening. The ship's doctor appeared and hurried off with the two men.

The line of departing passengers slowly inched forward.

Finally they were at the head of the departure line.

The captain tipped his hat. "I hope you all had a wonderful trip. Please join us again," he said in a thick Spanish accent.

"What was all the commotion?" Jinx asked innocently.

The captain pasted on a magnanimous smile. "Oh, a sick passenger. Nothing to worry about."

They walked down the gangplank and were finally on solid ground. Only to be caught up in the crush of waiting family and friends of the passengers.

"Look for a white Ford Explorer," Jinx said. "The keys will be inside."

Finally freeing themselves of the mass of people and luggage, they crossed the dock and hurried over the grass to the side of the street where cars were lined up.

They walked along the rows of cars until they found the Explorer.

"Is this it?" Jake asked.

Jinx walked up and tried the door. It opened. He hopped in and searched under the mat for the key. "Got it." He climbed out and opened the back doors, and they began loading their bags.

Jake got in and checked his watch. "We're scheduled to make the drop in an hour."

"We need to get somewhere out of sight so we can change," Rita said. "And we have to get the other cars."

"Let's get busy," Jake said, getting behind the wheel. His cell phone went off. He picked up the phone.

"Yeah."

"Do you have my merchandise?"

"We have it."

"Good. We'll be waiting. Look for a dark blue Taurus. And don't try anything. You'll regret it—I promise you."

The call disconnected.

Jake put the car in gear. He glanced over his shoulder. "You need to make that call now," he said to Jinx.

Lenora put the phone down on the bed. She'd still been unable to reach Traci. That worried her. Traci was supposed to be her eyes and ears from the airport to the ship, especially where Suarez was concerned. But there wasn't much she could do about it now. Knowing Traci, she'd turn up when it was time for her to get her cut.

They went back a long way, having met in college. For reasons that escaped them both, they clicked. Traci Jennings was gorgeous and knew it. She taught the petite and almost plain-Jane Lenora to make the most of her assets. How to use makeup and what clothes worked for her body. But there was always that gold-digger streak in Traci. Always out to make money, and she saw wealthy men as her avenue to financial freedom. The mechanics of the plan had been her idea, a way to set them free for good.

At first Lenora had balked, not wanting to get her hands that dirty. But the more Traci talked, the more it seemed possible. So they put the plan in place, and Lenora made that first phone call.

She'd had her moments of doubt along the way, but Traci had continued to whisper in her ear that they could pull it off without a hitch. So where was she?

"Did you talk to them?" Stan said, interrupting her thoughts.

She looked up at him, and her determination to free herself was renewed.

"Yes. Everything is going according to plan."

"Thirsty?" he asked, walking to the makeshift bar.

"Yes, a Coke with ice would be good."

Stan smiled.

The crew pulled onto a back street and jumped out.

"Okay, everyone straight on what needs to be done?" Eva asked.

"No room for fuckups," Jake said, pulling the duffle bag from the backseat. He tossed it into the car they'd pulled up alongside of.

"You two just don't screw up," Jinx said. "We'll be there." He and Rita got into the third car after a quick change.

"See you on the other side," Jake said, getting behind the wheel of his and Eva's vehicle.

The two cars pulled off, leaving the Explorer behind.

33

Jake braked to a stop on a side road on the outskirts of Miami. A few cars drove by, but none stopped.

"You sure this is the spot?" Eva asked.

Jake pulled out the map and compared it to the information on his GPS-equipped handheld. He looked around at the palm trees and the few abandoned buildings. "This is the spot."

"Then I guess we just have to wait."

Jake leaned his back against the headrest. "When this is over, I want to take a very long vacation."

Eva bit down on her bottom lip. She slowly shook her head as she looked out the passenger window. "I have a bad feeling."

Jake jerked his head in her direction. "Not again," he moaned.

"Something's not right."

If he'd listened to her bad feelings in the beginning, they wouldn't be sitting here, he thought.

"So what do you want to do?"

She frowned. "I don't know. I just get bad feelings—not peeks into the future."

"I think that's her," Jake said, his voice lifting in urgency.

Eva drew in a breath.

"You ready?"

She nodded.

The dark blue Taurus pulled to a stop.

Eva opened her door and got out. She opened the back door and took out the duffle bag.

The driver door opened, and she recognized Stan Ingram immediately. "Where's the wife?"

"I don't see a second passenger. Maybe she doesn't want you to put a face to her voice."

Eva swallowed. "Okay. Here goes. You ready?"

"Yep. Got my hand on the dial."

Eva slowly walked toward Stan. When she was a little more than a couple of feet in front of him, she could see that he was sweating bullets. He was scared.

She walked up to him. "It's all there."

His Adam's apple bobbed up and down. "You look d-different."

"Goes with the territory."

"Guess your p-plan didn't quite work out this t-time."

Eva bent her head to look in his car. "Where's wifey? I was really looking forward to meeting her," she said, dripping sarcasm.

He grinned. "S-she's resting. Little trick I l-learned from you."

Eva blanched when reality hit. "I see. Well enjoy the spoils. Our business is done." She turned to leave.

"Wait."

Eva stopped and slowly turned around. "What?"

He wiped his forehead. "S-something that's b-been bothering me." He swallowed. "D-id anything . . . ever h-happen that night?"

Eva rolled her eyes over his body. A slow smile moved across her mouth. "Why Stan, don't you remember?" She turned away and walked to the car without looking back and jumped in. "Little problem," she said, fastening her seat belt.

Jake started the engine. "What?"

"We aren't going to be able to tag both of them. Lenora's not in the car."

"Damn. Maybe that was the bad feeling you were talking about." He watched Stan pull off from his side view mirror.

"Let Jinx and Rita know. Don't want them to be surprised," Eva said. "Stan's not so innocent as he pretends to be."

Jake made the call to Jinx and brought him up to speed. "Everything else ready? Good. We'll meet you in an hour. Call me when it's done." He disconnected the call and pulled off.

Stan was so elated, his hands shook even as he gripped the wheel. When he figured he was far enough away, he pulled over to the side of the road.

He looked around before he unzipped the bag. His heart slammed in his chest. On top was an oversize clear plastic bag filled with diamonds. Underneath were stacks of brand-new one-hundred-dollar bills, neatly held together by rubber bands. Mesmerized, he slowly lifted the plastic bag and opened it. He took out a handful and stared at their beauty. He was rich beyond his wildest imagination. He would never have thought that all this was on the receiving end of his wife's little scheme. Now, he could buy love. He wouldn't have to beg for it or grovel for it again. And there had to be at least . . .

Flashing lights filled the interior of the car, bouncing off the diamonds and turning them into brilliant cuts of red and blue.

A sudden sharp tap on his window caused him to drop his bounty in his lap. His head snapped to the side. A police officer was leaning down into his window with a billy club in his hand. Another officer came up on his other side. The officer on his side signaled for him to roll down his window.

"License and registration."

Stan fumbled for his wallet and more of the diamonds slid between his legs onto the floor of the car.

"Please step out of the car, sir," the officer said. "And keep your hands where I can see them."

"B-but I was . . ."

"Step out of the car," the second officer ordered.

Once he was out of the car, the first officer pulled him to the front of the vehicle while the second officer inspected the car. Slowly the officer stood up with diamonds in one hand and a fist full of green in the other.

"You want to explain all that?" the first officer asked.

Stan's throat was so dry and tight, he couldn't get the words out without choking on them.

"I-I'm a businessman. H-here on business."

"Is that right? What kind of business would have you transporting what looks like diamonds and a bag full of money on a Miami highway?"

"I . . ."

"You can explain everything down at the precinct. I'm sure they'll sort everything out. Turn around, please."

Stan did as he was told. His arms were drawn behind him, and the cold metal of the handcuffs wrapped around his wrists. The officer ushered him to the backseat of the police car.

The other officer took the bag from the front seat and put it in the trunk of the police car and got in beside his partner.

"Did you call the impound?"

"Yeah, they're on their way to pick up the car."

The police car pulled off. They drove for about twenty minutes before pulling up in front of the Miami Police Department. The officers got out of the car and took Stan inside the precinct along with the bag from the trunk.

They brought him over to a bench and told him to sit down.

He'd never been so terrified in his life. How could he have been so careless as to stop and open the bag on the road? Oh, God—he was going to jail. But he wasn't going alone. He'd tell everything he knew from that night in the hotel right up to when he drugged his wife.

He watched one handcuffed suspect after another be carted in and out of the precinct. Metal clanging against metal provided background music in concert with ringing telephones, barked orders, and cries of "I didn't do it."

Stan glanced up at the clock on the wall. He'd been sitting there for almost two hours. Where were those cops?

34

Jake and Eva pulled up to the landing strip and parked the car in the back.

"They should be here any minute," Eva said, looking around.

Jake got out of the car. "I told him to call me when it was done." He paced back and forth in front of the car.

"Maybe he couldn't for some reason."

"Like what reason? Like trouble? You got any more of those bad feelings?"

Eva folded her arms. "He's your brother."

"She's your cousin."

"Then I guess we wait," Eva said.

Jake leaned against the side of the car. He looked at Eva. "How are you feeling?"

She shrugged a little, a half smile on her face. "Not bad. Guess that morning sickness thing hasn't fully kicked in."

Jake nodded. "What if it's a girl?"

"What if it's a boy?" She moved in front of him and stood in between his legs.

He hooked his arms around her waist. "Scary."

"Yeah, scariest thing we've ever done."

"Yeah." He lowered his head for a quick kiss when the short blast of a car horn snapped them apart.

"No time for all that lovey-dovey stuff," Jinx said, striding from the car. Rita hopped out from the other side.

"Well, don't you two look impressive in your little uniforms," Eva joked.

Jinx did a short bow. "Miami's finest."

"Got the stuff?" Jake asked.

Jinx held up the duffle bag, identical to the one they took from Stan's car. He grinned. "Poor old Stan. They're gonna book him on a bag of dirty laundry."

They all broke out laughing.

"Come on. Let's get out of here," Rita said. "These polyester pants are killing me."

Lenora's head pounded. She tried to open her eyes but quickly shut them against the light. The pounding continued. But it wasn't her head. It was the door. She struggled to sit up.

"Mrs. Ingram. Open the door. It's the police."

Lenora blinked several times, shook her head to clear it. She looked around. Where was Stan?

"Mrs. Ingram! Open the door."

Lenora pushed herself to a standing position. She felt sick. She made it to the door and pulled it open. Two uniformed officers stood in front of her with Stan in handcuffs.

"What's going on? Why is my husband in handcuffs?"

"He had a very interesting story to tell us, *Agent* Ingram. Why don't you get your things and come with us."

"I want to call my supervisor. I . . . I'm on special assignment."

"We've been in touch with your supervisor, Agent Flannagan. He doesn't know about any special assignment. Come with us, ma'am."

She whirled on Stan with fear and fury. "What did you tell them? You fool! What did you say?" She lunged at him.

The officer stepped in between them and took her by the arm. "Get your things, ma'am." He motioned to an officer near a second patrol car. "Secure the room."

Lenora got her purse and shoes and was led out of the motel room.

35

"So how did we make out?" Rita asked as she reapplied her lipstick. She took a look out of the airplane window.

"I figure minus a couple of handfuls of real diamonds and about ten grand in cash, chalking those up to operating expenses, we cleared close to a mil," Jake said.

Jinx whistled. "How sweet it is."

Eva looked at the team. "Me and Jake could have never pulled this off without you. You didn't have to get involved, but you did—and we appreciate it." She turned to Jake and squeezed his hand.

"That's what family is for," Rita said.

"When we land in Honolulu, I'm going straight to the beach," Jake announced.

Eva's eyes widened in surprise. "Jake?" she softly questioned.

He leaned in close to her. "When I said I was going to

put the past behind me, I really meant it. Might as well get started." He kissed her lightly. She rested her head on his shoulder and smiled.

ONE MONTH LATER

Sebastian looked up. Tara was standing in the doorway of his office.

"This box just came for you." She walked in and put it on his desk.

"Thanks," he murmured.

"Still no word from Eva?"

"No." He sighed. He'd gotten a phone call from her several weeks earlier, which he'd told no one about. She'd told him that she was sorry about running out on him, that she loved him and not to worry about her. He hadn't heard from her since.

Tara hesitated a moment and then walked out.

Sebastian looked at the box, hesitating before pulling it toward him. He picked it up. It was kind of light. There was no return address, and the postmark had been smeared by the relentless rain.

He took a letter opener from the cup on his desk and cut through the tape that sealed it shut. There was an envelope on top.

He took it out and opened it.

Dear Bass,

I can't tell you how much I miss you, but I am doing well. There is so much about me that you don't know,

*and it's best that you never do. I've enclosed a little
something that I hope will help you to get the second
location up and running.*

  *Maybe we will see each other again one day. But
even if we don't, know that you will always be in my
heart.*

  Love,
  Eva

He reread the letter and then slowly put it to the side.
He peeled away the stuffing in the box and gasped when
the contents were revealed.

There had to be at least fifty thousand dollars in brand-
new bills—if not more.

Mesmerized, he picked up a neat stack and held it in his
hand. He didn't want to think or imagine where the money
had come from and how Eva had gotten hold of it.

She was right. There were things about her that he
didn't know. He shoved the money back into the box and
sealed it. And some things were best left in the dark.

"Hey, babe, I'm going for a swim," Jake called out.

They'd secured a small house on the big island and
were living a life of luxury. Their needs were small, and
they had enough money to do whatever they wanted. Eva
wanted to start her own small boutique business and had
begun seeking supplies. Jake did computer repair when the
mood hit him, and Jinx and Rita had decided that the same
beautiful weather every day of the year was mind-numbing
and had decided to take a tour of Europe, promising to be
back for the arrival of the baby.

"Okay," she called from the kitchen. "I'll have lunch ready when you get back."

The phone rang. Eva crossed the ceramic-tiled kitchen floor to the phone that hung on the wall.

"Hello."

"Did you think I would not find you?"

Shit. Her heart stumbled in her chest. "Who is this?"

"Oh, I think you know. I want my money back, and my diamonds."

"I don't know what you're talking about."

"Well, while you are figuring it out, you have one month to return what belongs to me. I told you that night that I would have given you anything you wanted. You didn't have to steal from me. I will be in touch."

The call disconnected.

How could he know? He'd never seen her. Truth slammed her in the chest. *"I told you that night . . ."* He thought she was Rita.

"I forgot a towel," Jake said, walking back into the room. He stopped short. "Babe, what is it?" He came up to her, clasped her shoulders. "Are you sick?"

"He knows. He found us."

"Who?"

She looked up into his eyes. "Suarez." She shivered. "And just when I was getting used to lounging for a living."

"How in the world did he find us?"

"I don't have a clue."

"Well, didn't you get one of your funny feelings or something?"

"All this damned sunshine and blue skies must have burned out my sensors," she snapped.

Jake twisted his mouth, ran his hand across his hair. "How much of what we took do we have left?"

"Not enough to keep him from really being pissed off."

Jake pulled out a chair and sat down. "Hmmm, looks like we're gonna have to pull another job."

Eva took a seat opposite him. A slow smile crept across her mouth. Her eyes got that old sparkle. "I was getting bored with all this sunshine anyway."

"I thought I'd never hear you say that!" He smiled in delight, that old surge of energy setting his veins on fire.

Eva leaned forward. "So what we need is a plan. And I was thinking . . ."

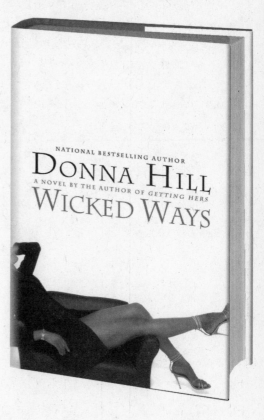